maxwell empire

maxwell empire

BOOKS 1 AND 2

MAXWELL PARTINGTON

To order additional copies of this book, contact:
Xlibris
1-800-455-039
www.Xlibris.com.au
Orders@Xlibris.com.au
801943

MAXWELL EMPIRE

BOOK 1

TABLE OF CONTENTS

CHAPTER 1

Rusty eats Uncle Malcolm

Dad, Uncle Malcolm is going.

Sorry, Davey, but he has had his time here and must go.

But I love him.

Me too, but with his brain not working it is no longer him we talk to.

But Rusty could be eating him.

Well, last year it was Aunty Joan who could have been in Rusty's bowl.

I don't want to be in Rusty's bowl.

Davey, you are bright and fit and a good worker. It will be years before you are in Rusty's bowl.

I just never want him eating me.

You know that if we want to have a pet we must agree to be pet food when we go. It is what we have to do to have a pet.

Judy has a budgie and she isn't going to be food for him.

Well, budgies don't eat meat. So we don't need to harvest meat to feed them.

I don't want to be harvested.

You know that for that to happen your brain will have changed so you don't know what is going on. It is not as though people being harvested know they are becoming pet food.

Well that is not right. Baddies know.

Just as well. They are criminals and deserve to know they are going to be in Rusty's bowl tomorrow. After they have been processed anyway.

I guess it helps keep people good.

It surely is something that you would have on your mind if you were thinking of being bad.

Dad, do they process baddies if they are full of drugs?

That's a thought. I guess they don't. Not for pet food anyway. It might upset the pets.

What would they do with them then?

Davey, remember we watched that hunt episode last week. You know where they were in the Blue Mountains, that really pretty country near Sydney.

Yes. It was exciting. They could not find him. He hid behind the rocks all the time.

And the trees. Still, they eventually got a good sight on him and that was the end of it. Now he was fit. Not on drugs. He had been a druggie. I guess they cleaned it out of his system so he could try to get away. Not that he did. But he would be okay for Rusty to have in his bowl.

Well, I know animals have as many rights as humans but I really don't like the idea of Uncle Malcolm being in Rusty's bowl.

So how about Judy's Polo? He won't live forever. When he dies he could be in Rusty's bowl. What do you think about that?

Dad! Pet pigs are not the same as uncles. I know they have the same rights but I can't say I feel the same about Polo as I do about Uncle Malcolm.

One thing. You can play Uncle Malcolm's hologram any time you like to see him again, talking and carrying on. And with Aunty Joan.

Some people keep holograms of their pets. I don't think Judy does though. Have you thought of keeping one of Rusty, Dad?

Not at all Davey. We love to cuddle our pets because they can't talk to us. People talk and sing and we can watch and listen to them forever. You can't cuddle up to a hologram. It just would be a bit of waving your arms around in the air.

Is there a hunt on this week, Dad?

Good idea, Davey. I had forgotten that this week it is a big one. Four baddies in Lagos. The bits that are out of the water at all are out of bounds but I don't think there will be any places can't be used. So many places to hide. All those places under water. Most of the city is under water. Make sure we have lots of stuff to eat because it is going to take a long time before they are killed.

It will be the middle of the night here. I hope I don't go to sleep.

Don't worry Davey. I will make sure to wake you up when they are in sight.

Thanks Dad. I am going to bed now. Night.

Good night, Davey.

CHAPTER 2

Space City factory Spaceship visit

Scott and Simon are in Space City and are about to visit the Spaceship factory. They have had breakfast and have joined the day's group tour over the facility. The group is moving along the Observation Tube of the Spaceship factory to see the spaceship Maxwell 09 being built. The Observation Tube is air filled and warm but they wear spacesuits as a precaution against something going wrong. They wear magnetic boots because they are weightless and it makes moving along the corridor more comfortable. The Space factory viewing corridor has iron plates to step along so the magnet bottomed boots hold you to the iron plated pathways. The electromagnets in the boots are turned on when the foot is descending and off when the foot is ascending. They are attached to the guide rail because there is no gravity in the Tube and while they can drift readily along it their attachment stops them interfering with the other members of the group.

They are looking at the spaceship.

What about that? It is huge. Says Simon, who wants to work in research.

See all those blocks of ice. Having a temperature out there in the shade of lower than minus one hundred degrees Celsius means water is only in the form of ice. Said Scott.

But how many blocks? There look to be thousands of them.

They add up to three thousand tonnes. So at a tonne each that is three thousand ice blocks.

Well, it doesn't look like a spaceship from the stories we read as kids.

It's out of the atmosphere. It just has to have the bits hang together.

That is just right. Those blocks of ice are just strung together with cables.

And then when it needs to put them in its fusion motor it just drags them over to it.

For a robot it is just plain huge.

It says here that it will weigh six thousand tonnes and then there will be the extra three thousand tonnes of water making a total of nine thousand tonnes.

Maxwell 09 is going to take over seven thousand years to get to its planet. That is thirty nine light years away.

We won't be visiting our rellies for a weekend visit.

Just to have a conversation means waiting seventy eight years after saying Hello to hearing their How are you?

When does it leave?

In 4615. It was going to be 4215 but they stopped making spaceships for a few hundred years to hear how Maxwell 01 had got on.

There would be a few changes I guess. It will be twelve hundred years after Maxwell 01 left so they must have better space elevator cables or computers or whatever.

It is nearly three hundred years since Maxwell 01 arrived. Even with a conversation taking eight years or so between saying Hello and hearing How are you? That boils down to a lot of conversations.

Maxwell 01 sent a message every year. I wonder if Maxwell 09 will do that. It is a lot of messages saying I have been having a good sleep.

Yes. Over seven thousand of them. After five years of acceleration the spaceships just head towards their planet before they have five years of deceleration to then orbit the planet.

I guess it will be a bit less deceleration because they used up over a million tonnes of water accelerating so they have less weight to slow down.

Yes. Maxwell 09 will calculate it so it so it goes into orbit around its planet at the right speed.

The cables holding the ice blocks will then be used to make the Space Elevator to the surface of Maxwell 09.

While the Space Elevator is made it will be getting the airships set up to go down to the surface to start spreading algae spores all over the planet to make oxygen.

It will send down some mining robots as well to find the minerals it needs to make more robots, to set up a Space City and to make more Space Elevators.

Actually there must be a lot of mining robots.

The airships are needed to change the atmosphere of the planet for humans to live outside the domes it will build but mining robots are needed to find the minerals it needs and then to mine them and then to send them up the Space Elevator to it for processing.

Look at him. He's jetting around to do his job all over the place. Humans would need a huge spacesuit on to be out there.

Talk about sexist. I guess robots in the kitchen are her while robots in factories are him.

Sorry. But saying it all the time gets me. I say him for all of them.

Right. It's him. He certainly zooms around the place without the need to safety belts or any other safety equipment.

Robots will have built all the spaceships. If the job is particularly tricky a human guided robot can be used with the human safely in warm, air conditioned comfort.

That is what the woman was doing back there. She had the visor on and was waving her arms about. I thought she was dancing or something.

We have passed a few of them. Most of the time the robots can do it all on their own. I suppose it could be a problem when it gets to Maxwell 09.

Maxwell 01 did not report any robot problems. Those ones designed for starting new human homes must be better quality.

Humans are not needed much in manufacturing. People I know who want to work are looking at research or design.

When Maxwell 09 parks itself over the equator and starts to deploy its Space Elevator it would be thinking it needs a better material for the job. That is what I want to find. A better Space Elevator material.

Since they discovered the material we use now and that is over a thousand years ago I don't know you will find one.

I will try anyway.

I don't know that I will have a job. Not full time anyway. With the Government paying everyone whether they work or not I like the idea of a lot of time off. I think some of the Education Inputs could be improved so I will work on that.

You will be working online so you could be on the Earth, in Space City, or on the Moon.

Yes. On the Moon I can take a break in the gym and see just how many metres I can get off the floor. But it would be a shortish stay. Low gravity is not good for bones.

So Space City would be even shorter.

Not really. The artificial gravity from the rotation of the living areas means you have Earth gravity. You had that before we came out here. So I could be here forever. Not that I would want to. Earth is too beautiful to stay away from it.

I must say I will be getting out of my lab to hike in the forests. Where there are no people. Can you imagine how crowded Earth must have been with over fifteen billion people? Just as well China went up in the air.

Yes. I love the forests. But I love all that is in our life.

I cannot think of a better time to be alive.

Robots to do all the work, humans to do all the play.

What about those robots. What do you think they are making?

That must be a DNA store. It is being surrounded by ice blocks to protect it from flying objects on its journey. Try to anyway. They evidently have half a dozen DNA stores around the spaceship to make sure they get all eight million or so sets of DNA to the new Earth environment. With a journey of at least eight hundred years they need to protect the reason for going. With Maxwell 09 it needs to be protected for over seven thousand years.

I wonder if they are taking DNA of bindii and double gees and mosquitoes. I can imagine leaving those ones behind.

If they have the DNA they take it. Earth 1, 2, 3, 4, 5, 6, 7, 8, 9, 10 must be all the same as Earth original. In the beginning anyway.

So we have three thousand one tonne iceblocks around six DNA sets. That is five hundred blocks per DNA set. Have we seen ice block making?

They pump water up to several kilometres above the Earth and then into plastic bags which are kept in the shade and will be at a temperature well below freezing so that big cubes of plastic covered ice are formed. These can then be taken up the Space Elevator to the spaceship. They are covered with more plastic coating to make sure no water is lost on the journey to the planet they are headed for. At the spaceship we have seen them stacking the water cubes and securing them with ties.

Right. Losing water would be losing the ability to slow down to meet the planet, so the water is very important. And the plastic is used in the Space Elevator.

The water in the fusion motor gets ionised and pushes the spaceship to a speed of about one and a half million metres per second in five years. Then after eight hundred years Maxwell 01 turned around and took five years or so to slow down to go into orbit around Maxwell 01, over the equator.

So eventually Maxwell 01 will be like Earth with Space City a ring around above the equator, with Space Elevators to the surface from the Space City.

Even if we made Maxwell 01 Mark 2 big enough to support humans it would be about thirty generations before it got there. What would be the point?

Yes. No point. When humans are old enough on Maxwell 01 we can say Hello and eight years later we can hear their How are you? And then we can say I am fine. How are you? And eight years later we will hear their I am fine, but I don't think they will ask What is the weather like today? Conversations as such are pretty well ruled out.

Anyway, what about this spaceship. It leaves in thirty nine years so there must be a lot more to get built.

The motors must be going way down there. I guess they have not started on that part yet. That is one of the projects I could work on. Better fusion motors.

The movies just have no idea. This is just a huge network of bits to hang other bits on until they are needed, like the ice blocks.

Not having humans makes it completely different. This huge robot doesn't need enclosed spaces to hold air so it is just rigging. With the temperature in space three degrees Kelvin it had better be able to stand it for seven thousand years.

The main problem is always the acceleration but with a mass of nine million kilograms that will be very small. Its biggest problem will be turning around.

Yes, but it has seven thousand years to do that so I don't see that is a problem either.

True. So perhaps its biggest problem is the unforeseen comet or other object we don't know about. But space has lots of space so I guess the chances of encountering any object are pretty low.

That is where Maxwell 01 had an advantage. Being the nearest star meant not much chance of finding anything on the way there.

The plastic from the ice blocks will help make enclosed areas for the robots it has to do their work when it gets to Maxwell 09. They will need to have something so they can set up the airships and mining robots to send down to the surface along the Space Elevator.

And they will need somewhere to work on the Space Elevator before they do that.

The robots have programs which have to last seven thousand years. So the program is stored on DNA. So a change on the DNA and we have EXTERMINATE EXTERMINATE Darleks. I do love Dr Who, even if it is from three thousand years ago or so.

I think we need to get in the fast lane to get to the food court and watch the Earth from up here. I don't like eating without gravity so much but I do like seeing Earth while I eat.

Good idea.

After lunch we should go to the Observation Deck to have a good look at the Earth. The telescopes are very good.

I agree. Food for the tummy then food for the soul.

CHAPTER 3

Hearing from Maxwell 01

Did you see it on the news? We heard again from Maxwell 01 today. Said Kevin.

What did they have to say? Asked Julie.

They are ready to start making animals. They have the DNA for all our animals. With the plants doing well the next step is animals. And then humans.

Just as well they won't expect a reply. It wouldn't get there for four years.

Four years isn't long for them. They left for Maxwell 01 in 3415. It took 800 years or so to get there so they would have been in orbit in 4200 or thereabouts.

Just as well they are robots and not humans. Those times are a bit long for humans.

True, but they send a message at regular intervals but if you are not doing anything for hundreds of years there is not much to talk about. And now they have more to talk about than setting up camp on Maxwell 01.

Well it is 4576 now so it took it about 300 years to set up the space elevator and then get everything going up and down to the surface. They set up a dome to begin the birth of humans and other animals. And fill it with a suitable atmosphere of course.

The robots they took would be getting on. Yes, they would be making replacement robots in the spaceship.

The ones that got there first would be worn out. Actually I guess there must be a lot of messages about new robots being made.

No doubt. And it would have kept a record of its progress. The trouble is of course when we ask it for a particular copy of the record of an activity it will take us eight years to get it from Maxwell 01.

I should assume it was set up to send us a complete history of the progress. Much of it would not make interesting TV watching.

I look forward to hearing from humans.

If humans haven't started to be produced it will be a while before we hear from them. We'll just hear from robots for years yet.

CHAPTER 4

China meteorite 01

mum, the question is "Was the 2091 meteorite strike on China a good thing?". What do you think?

Well, Sammy, it is really a question for you to consider. You have had all the information about that time input at your last session. What do you think?

Well, it reduced the world's population by a half or so. But I would not have liked to starve to death. Or been killed fighting for food. Or fighting to get to the southern hemisphere.

Yes, that was really an asteroid hitting the Earth. A huge one. So there was no sunshine in the northern hemisphere for over two years. China and India still used coal to make electricity while the rest of the world used solar panels. No sun meant no electricity. China and India could use electricity to grow food in factories but China kept it for the Government and army. When people found out they rebelled and killed them all.

So the meteorite killed many people and animals and plants but it meant the start of the World Government. That was good.

Yes, it was good. No more Chinese wanting to rule the world.

The southern hemisphere got a lot more people from the north.

Yes, with ninety percent of the population in the northern hemisphere any sort of boat that could get you south was used to move people. Many countries tried to stop it but it was useless. Europeans flooded into Africa. Asians headed to Africa or Australia. North Americans to the south. If you couldn't move you probably died.

Australia got a lot. The Australian Aboriginals got upset with people turning up on land they thought was theirs. After they killed a whole lot of refugees and got a whole lot of themselves killed Australia said the land belonged to all Australians.

Lawyers had made a great deal of money from the land rights cases. You will get that input in two sessions time. Also they could not afford to have Aboriginals treated as a disadvantaged group seeing they had been like that for three hundred years and not improved. Not with so many really disadvantaged people. Australians were now all the same.

Africa was advantaged getting so many Europeans to get the countries working properly. Corruption had to reduce. Industry had to increase. The population was kept under control by allowing only one or two children per couple. There were many people killed by those not wanting to share their country. But the whole place became one. Like the African version of the European Union.

The Europeans brought their weapons with them. It was like when the British fought the Sudanese in the nineteenth century before when seven hundred British died and thirty thousand Sudanese died. The ratio was the same in the twenty first century. The first factories they built were for guns. The continent had been colonised by the Europeans before and now they were back.

There were now less humans. The world could bring all those animals and plants wiped out by too many humans back.

Yes, the storing of the DNA of all plants and animals in space before the asteroid strike meant that a method of restoring all plants and animals was possible.

Humans had been a big problem eating many other living things out of existence.

Yes, you would not have thought such an event could be a good thing. It is too bad humans did not do anything about there being too many of them before it.

Scientists found ways to use the DNA to bring them all back. It was good because when they thought of sending a spaceship to Maxwell 01 they needed to be able to make it like Earth with all the same animals and plants.

It took over a thousand years to get the spaceship to be able to do all the things necessary to make Maxwell 01 another Earth.

Well, because they had not got the space elevators at that time it had to wait a thousand years for that. Once they had the space elevators they could build the spaceships.

And they needed the fusion rocket engine. Getting water to move fast enough to get the spaceship moving at a high enough speed to get to Maxwell 01 in eight hundred years.

Maxwell 01 used to have a different name because it was around the nearest star to Earth at four point two light years. The Maxwell Government will have the Maxwell Empire formed in another ten thousand years or so; well the first ten Maxwell planets anyway.

By then maybe Maxwell 01 will have fixed the atmosphere so humans can go walking in the countryside. It must be not so good to be in a dome all the time because the air is not breathable.

Well, they could breathe it but it would kill them. They need the plants to hurry up and photosynthesise enough so the carbon dioxide is changed to oxygen.

And then they can get all the animals they have the DNA for made so it is like Earth.

Yes, all the millions of species. They could have called it Earth 02 instead of Maxwell 01.

I hope the humans have the brains to not think they are better than other animals and breed without regard for the other animals so that there is standing room only for animals and they are all humans.

Our ancestors unfortunately had religions that thought just that. Humans were something better than the other animals. They could not control the number of humans when they had that idea. Just as well that we now have the Octet.

Some of the religions had the right idea. The Sioux Indians in North America had humans as being on the same level as the other animals. And the Buddhists believed you had to do the right thing by animals because you could be reincarnated as any one of them.

I think we have got off the subject a bit. We need to talk about it later because we need to get on with making dinner.

THE OCTET

Live your life with the knowledge that this time you have alive is all that you are going to get, with no previous life having been had by you or that there will be another life after you die, so value this life.

Humans are social animals so enjoy and value time spent together with other animals, particularly those of your species.

This life is all you are going to have so value it. Do not cause society to remove your life from you because of your conduct.

Look after the well-being of your mind and body.

Take full responsibility for your actions.

One should treat others as one would like others to treat oneself.

All living things have a right to exist and all animals are equal.

Value the future on a timescale longer than your own.

CHAPTER 5

Bus to Moon City

What event are you in? asked Kailee.

Jimmy snorted. Event! event! I am in six events. Three on the snow and three track and field.

Sorry! I didn't know you were such a star, admonished Kailee.

Sorry. Getting a bit up myself I suppose, said Jimmy.

Is anyone else going from Albury?

Yeah, a lot. We have sixteen in different events and then some parents are coming. And the coaches of course.

Is it costing much?

It's all covered by our sports allowance, thank goodness. Otherwise I could not afford to go.

Will you be away long?

A total of twenty one days. It takes a while to get there and then we compete for five days. Then we have a look at Moon City and the surface.

Do you get to walk on the surface?

Yeah, but only for an hour. If you want longer they charge more than our allowance and none of us can afford it.

When do you leave?

We fly to the Indonesia 2 Space Elevator on Saturday. We are booked to go up right away to Space City and we get on the Moon bus on Tuesday night.

I would love to see the Earth from the Moon.

Me too. I am really looking forward to being up there and looking back to see you. I will wave.

Ha, ha. Growled Kailee.

Don't you remember? We looked at the TV at Jenny's cousin who works up there and he waved at the camera. He waved for all of us to see. He must have had a sore arm by the time he done all his waving.

I remember. I just need you to get someone to video you so I can see you. I think you can phone me and show me you are waving and I will wave back.

Danny's coming. I will get him to hold my phone as I wave so you can see it.

Danny is going! I thought he was grounded.

Yeah. He is, or was. He is just such a star with his gymnastics that they think he will wipe the floor in his events. He is in all events for his age group.

Thank goodness your events will all be broadcast here on Earth. We can all see you flying way up in the air as you do your jumps and twists and turns and whatever.'

Those videos we saw of the snow jumps in the Moon were pretty spectacular. I hope we get to do as well. I don't know if we would be as good as those guys. They have been up there a long time and got used to jumping in the low gravity.

Don't knock your head on the roof.

You saw how big those jump spaces that they have dug out are. Huge. It would be impossible to hit the roof unless you had movers on your legs. Gold mines on Earth have big spaces underground but the ones on the Moon are enormous

I guess so. You used movers when you went in the races at Space City last year, didn't you?

Yes. Only small ones. They did not allow us to use the larger ones as we were not used to them. You saw the older guys on TV and they were really motoring. Jenny's big brother is really good with them.

But he did not win. Some of those guys were just so quick. A guy called Samantha won all the races she was in. We all want to be as good as she is.

I had better get home for dinner. Make sure you remember to phone me and wave to me from up there.

I will for sure Kailee. You could always get your mum to hold your phone so I can see you waving back.

Will do. Bye, Jimmy.

Bye, Kailee.

CHAPTER 6

Scott and Simon are looking at the Earth from a Space City Observation Deck at 130 degrees East.

Australia is all green now but most of it used to be brown because it was dry. You remember that thousands of years ago they had droughts when there had not been rain so their animals died or they sold them all off and gave up farming. Now it is all that beautiful green. Said Simon.

Robots were the answer, and the need to try to absorb carbon dioxide. See that sea going right up through the middle. Robots dug that. Australia is a pretty flat place anyway and they needed to grow more forest all over the planet. So they dug a sea, put in desalination plants by the million serviced by robots, and poured water all over the country. Explained Scott.

Of course having sea levels about twenty metres higher because of global warming helped.

True. They will need to shift the desalination plants if it is going to rise sixty metres or so as they suggest.

Yes, this was after the China impact so there were a lot less people but the warming problem kept getting worse.

So they grew trees, everywhere. So far the trees have not fixed things up but in another thousand years or so it will be green and the sea level will be going down.

And then your several greats grandchildren will go to London on foot and not in a robotic single person submersible.

Do you remember the story from Australian ancient history? Before the British arrived the Aborigines wars were usually about women. Wanting them back after they had gone to be with a man in another tribe or whatever, even after they arrived. You can read the accounts from those people from the First Fleet telling the same sort of stories. Aborigines did not have stories to read because they did not have writing, just oral history. Anyway, what better war to have than one where you get a woman and also a Toyota Landcruiser.

You must have read that yourself. It could not have been part of one of my History Stages or I would know that.

With the beginning of robots in manufacturing in the twenty first century in Australia a lot of Aboriginal men along the Murray River, you can see it along the middle of the telescope view, Albury is the big city near the Eastern end, the water shown there is quite big, it is the Hume, your many, many greats grandmother went sailing there.

Yes, that ancestor was a good sportswoman. Into soccer particularly. And small bore rifle shooting.

On the other side of Australia in the north west a tribe was about to get vast amounts of money from mineral rights and a huge claim was being settled. The guys in the east needed women, a job, or money, and these guys in the west had both. What better way to get it all than to engage in a bit of old time Aboriginal culture and take the women and the money. How to do it? A fishing trip.

With the Eastern seaboard next door so to speak that is a long way to go to catch fish.

The fishing was the excuse to get together with the locals. The guys from the east towed a caravan of boats they had borrowed to go fishing with their new buddies from the west. They had enough boats to hold all the men with a claim on the money. Off they all went to sea. When you go fishing you want a drink.

Definitely one of the things everyone I know does when they go fishing is have an Esky of ice cold stubbies with you. One of the things that hasn't changed over the centuries.

It is a bit of a problem if your drink has had something added to it to put you to sleep. Obviously the eastern guys did not go to sleep. They tossed the western guys overboard to wake them up, or so they told the guys rellies. Oh look. A million sharks are having breakfast on our friends. Get them back. Oh, too hard. The sharks have eaten them all.

I remember that Aboriginal culture was regarded as something that should be respected. I guess that is how these guys got away with it.

So now the east guys had heaps of women, money and hence new lives in the west. Actually they took the women and the money back east because the north west was as bad to live in as the east was good to live in. They could then buy their boats to go fishing on the Murray River with their new wives.

I remember one of my ancestors wanted an Aboriginal ancestor but he could only find a pile of convicts when he did his search. All the convicts were from Ireland but one of the convicts kids had married a soldier from England who was in charge of convicts. So they were a mixture of Irish and English.

The northern coastline of Australia shows big indents now that the sea level has gone up twenty metres. The west coast is going to have big problems if it keeps going up as much as they say but so far it is not too bad. Down south Melbourne has lost a bit to sea water.

So much for Australia. Up there in China they have made it all green as well. The western part used to have deserts and the high country had snow all the time. All that has been greened by pumping fresh water from the desalination plants in the east. A lot of rivers used to rely on the snow in the Himalayas but that is now not there all the time. It has been a problem they have fixed with robots and pumps.

See the huge crater in the middle of China. It is all green now but when it happened back in 2091 rock was strewn over a vast area of the country. And up in the air. That was the start of the Earth having a sensible population.

If you go to China you can visit the cities along the old east coast in a submersible. It will take you all around Shanghai and Tianjin or any of the other places now under water. It is at twenty metres now but it is supposed to keep rising and they think it might get to sixty metres. It just isn't stopping.

Those twentieth and twenty first ancestors of ours burning coal and oil have a lot to answer for. Apart from the crime of burning it at all. Your ancestors are also from China from above where Laos was so it is not under water. See how your ancestors from Thailand fared.

The middle bit you can see is under water. You can visit the Grand Palace in Bangkok in a submersible, and the dozens of temples from the Buddhist faith. The rellies were from the North East so it will never go under water.

When the sea rises to sixty metres if it does all the middle of Thailand will be under water. That is the best rice growing area. It is just as well the population has gone down so much otherwise we would all be hungry.

Yes, wait until we get over Europe. Some parts of that are under water completely now.

So we are off to see the next factory which makes communication fibre. Gravity is a problem for making it on Earth so they make it all up here.

That is in the non-gravity section. In the gravity section they have a huge number of vertical farms. Space City has farms all over the place. They even send fruit and vegetables down to the surface. We will have to have a good look at how they grow them all.

Good. We can have a sleep in the bus.

CHAPTER 7

Fred has a homework exercise

I have to discuss the benefits of the 2091 asteroid strike. Said Fred.
Have your friends done the work? Said his Mum.

Yes, but I was concentrating on getting my poems done for English.

Well, what do you think of it?

Humans were out of control by the end of the twenty first century. The expression breeding like rabbits is used in the text. We had stuff on rabbit plagues a couple of stages ago in science. There were just too many humans.

Yes, it's just as well the DNA of all our animals and plants was stored in space so we could bring them back from extinction.

In Stage 10D I do an experiment using stored DNA to reproduce life. Gary has done 10D and told me about the experiment.

So the quicker you finish the exercises for Biology Stage 10B the sooner you will be able to go to school and do the experiment.

I can't see that they would have stopped breeding. There would have been standing room only. Our ancestors were not sensible, Mum.

Well, some countries were trying to stop religions having their way. Developed countries did not have a problem as the people saw they needed to have fewer kids to have a good life style.

But they usually did not try to get poorer countries to have less kids.

One of the problems was charities getting money to keep kids alive in countries that just could not support them and so women had more kids.

The material I got at the last stage suggests they should have been using the money to make sure the women stopped having kids. It said they should have been providing contraceptives or operating on them so they could not have kids after two at the most. Also that they should have given a monthly wage to women who did not have more than two kids.

You will have the figures for population growth. There were too many humans by the end of the twenty first century.

The number of species that had become extinct because there were so many humans makes me wonder why they thought it was not a problem having so many humans.

They certainly did not act as though they cared about other animals.

With the elephants all disappearing I would have thought they would have realised there were too many humans.

The problem was no one took much notice of what was happening in Africa. It wasn't just the elephants that went but the rhinoceros, hippopotamus, giraffes and the gorillas were wiped out. Some species are forever extinct because their DNA was not obtained for storage which is really disappointing.

The birds varied in how they were affected. If they adapted to living with humans and eating their scraps they got on well. If they relied on wetlands or any other part of the environment that humans were mucking up they disappeared.

It is a huge advantage having only two billion humans so that we can have all the animals that were around before man stuffed things up.

You need to say humans. Someone will tell you that you are being sexist.

Yes, I guess women would have been even more responsible for the size of the population than the men. Have you thought about the effect of the number of humans and the Earth now going under water? Parts of it anyway.

Yes, but at present I only need to give a report on whether the asteroid was a good thing. I think it was good. Humans might have just kept on breeding until there was standing room only.

So at the end of the year you will go skiing, will you? January is the best month for it in Switzerland.

Yes, we are having a week there. We could go a bit later but it isn't guaranteed after January.

Your ancestors used to go near Canberra. It is too bad there is none in Australia these days.

When I did New Zealand in Stage 7 Geography they used to have snow and glaciers all year but they only sometimes get snow these days and that is in July, usually anyway.

Your dad and I will visit New Zealand to see your Uncle Dave when you go to ski. He is a bit poorly seeing Aunty Jean has had her Celebration of Life.

I thought her Celebration was outstanding. She had kept up to date with her holograms so when she did go we still had her there talking to us. And playing her guitar and singing. She sounded really good. Last Tuesday I was thinking of her and turned on her hologram singing the same song.

Dementia is still a problem for older folk. You would think by now they would have got a cure for it. I am glad if when you do have it you do not understand that your Celebration of Life is your departure.

Is the part of Auckland he is in going to be under water soon?

His bit of Otara is still out of the water but he is going to have to move. Most of Auckland will be under water if the sea does go up sixty metres. At present it is at twenty one metres.

What about Alfie down in Christchurch. Couldn't his dad stay with him?

Well, he could if Alfie's place was above water but Christchurch has sunk. Surely you saw that on the news. There has been a lot of it and how people have had to shift.

I think it must have happened during the week I was getting this stage.

Most of New Zealand will be above water. The World Government has a group down there getting new cities built.

Do they want to come here? Albury won't be going under water.

I did ask your uncle but he has been in New Zealand most of his life and he does not want to move.

Well, the people in Bangladesh have all moved. Just as well the World Government helped them. There are millions of them around here.

Yes, making Albury into a major manufacturing hub provided lots of jobs to people servicing the robots that are not too sophisticated. Service robots can do it but it gives people something to do.

When they get settled they will no doubt prefer to leave the servicing to the robots and do things for themselves.

Anyway you had better get your report done. You do realise billions died when the asteroid struck.

Yes, but humans had killed billions of other animals.

CHAPTER 8

4576 Chickens

Did your Dad make you watch the news? Asked Grant.

Yeah, but I don't know why they get excited about what happened four years ago. Said Dennis.

And not when it is all about chickens.

I guess they want the humans to be happy and eat chicken.

How long before they make humans now?

Well, it is May 23rd, 4576, our time, and they said they had chickens. The robots would have started making humans when they knew the chickens were doing well, so I guess that would be soon after. Say a month or two. Then nine months to gestate. We should hear in a year or so that they have humans, but that is about four years ago, so our rellies are now three years old.

Happy third birthday, dear Maxwell 01 boy, or girl, or boys or girls.

So how many do you think they would have made?

No idea. The Maxwell 01 mission people must know what they programmed the robots to do but it would depend on what the robots thought of the conditions on Maxwell 01.

I guess your dad made you watch the photo of the Plant Dome we got four years ago.

And the photos of the potatoes, corn, broccoli, tomatoes, turnips, and whatever else that arrived last year.

I've always wondered, why are the plants in a dome?

They produce oxygen which is needed by the animals so they grow them in domes and collect the oxygen. They did say that but it is four years ago.

I should have known that. I did the Biology Stage exercises well. My marks were good. The Science Stages I have been doing at a great rate.

What about the Maths Stages. They take me longer. But History is the big problem for me. They put in the material but my brain just does not want anything to do with it. I just cannot get all that excited about when the first Space Elevator went up on Earth, or the Moon, or Maxwell 01. It is all in there but getting it out is like having a traffic jam in my brain.

I like knowing about what happened before. I don't have any problem extracting it. Especially when it is about my ancestors.

Knowing about my ancestors is different. I can recall the material about them easily whether it is from the twentieth, thirtieth or fortieth centuries. I am pleased they know so much to put in.

It is too bad we do not know much before the nineteenth century.

Yes, the idea that people could not write is amazing.

It is one of the advantages of having convicts sent to Australia back then. The records show what they were in trouble for and what they did before they served their sentence.

The idea that the locals did not have writing is amazing. Only communication by speaking. Not a very reliable way to record history.

Well, the locals were still at the stone age.

A lot of Chinese would be unhappy about their records. When the asteroid hit back in 2091 it wiped out a huge area of China and everything in it.

Yes, if it had hit somewhere that had few people it would have had less impact.

Joke. The impact of the impact was bad for the Chinese and all the northern hemisphere. And the southern hemisphere as well.

The kids on Maxwell 01 will have records of all their ancestors and everyone else's.

With holograms of the more recent ones so they can see them walking and talking.

If they are three now when we know the day they were born we should send them a birthday message.

So it will be Happy Birthday, seven year old boys and girls.

I am looking forward to finding out when they were born. Do we say born if they are test tube babies?

It will be like the biblical tale of Adam and Eve. Only it took more than seven days or whatever.

I guess waiting four years is as bad as some of the explorers in olden times. If they were in a sailing ship they were away from home for several years and did not know when their wife had their baby.

With the mortality rates in those times it could be that the child had been born, lived a while and then died before dad knew anything.

Actually, we are in a similar situation. It takes us four years before we get the news from Maxwell 01. In that time they might have all died or built more domes and increased the population by tens or hundreds or even thousands.

One thing about it, making more people with test tubes sure does speed things up.

Let's hope they have the brains to limit the females to two kids at the most when they do start breeding naturally. If it had not been for the asteroid the Earth would have been all humans only.

Yes, just as well they saved DNA from all the plants and animals. That was one of the problems with religions.

The number of species wiped out by too many humans was in the hundreds of thousands. If the asteroid had not stopped human growth it would have been worse.

Being able to use the stored DNA to make the extinct species again was a huge relief. What humans had destroyed they could then fix up.

And we could have humans throughout the universe. We will have ten spaceships so far heading off to start new Earths but eventually humans will be everywhere. They will all know their history even if they are like you and have trouble relating to it.

Well Maxwell 10 will be better off getting the information about their history from the data stored on the DNA memory chips because they will ask us a question and send it to us but they will probably have died when the answer arrives because the time between asking the question and getting a reply is eighty years.

Yes, being forty light years away is difficult. What about in a million years or so and humans are on the other side of our galaxy. They will ask Earth a question and get their answer in one hundred and forty thousand years. I guess they won't be asking Earth anything. Just as well they will have the recordings so they know their origins.

CHAPTER 9

Bus to Moon City 2

After Jimmy said goodbye to Kailee he went home and finished packing for his trip to the Lunar Olympics. He was only allowed one suitcase so he was making sure that he had clothes that he could easily wash and that did not need ironing. There would be lots of help when he got to the Moon but there were always delays in getting garments back so he preferred to look after his clothes on his own. Robots could do a better job but he could not afford to have to wait for them to do the job. If he lived on the Moon it would be different or if the Sports Committee had allowed him to take more luggage. He could understand the need to keep the weight down but one suitcase was a real problem.

The group met at the Albury Airport and boarded the direct rocket flight to the Space Elevator. Albury was an important research centre in the development of new materials for space travel and planet terraforming so there was considerable traffic of both scientists and planners and their families. The rocket landed in the Space Port in Sumatra and they booked into a hotel while they waited for their pod which would transfer the group to the Space City.

Hi Kailee. It's Jimmy. Did I wake you?

Jimmy! Where are you?

We've just got to the Space Port and we should be going up to Space City tomorrow. Evidently it depends on how much material is coming down from the Space City to the surface but at present Earth factories need a lot of platinum they processed from an asteroid on the Moon and have shipped to Space City for it to get down to the surface so there is a lot of traffic going up.

So you will be up there tomorrow night, will you?

Probably. The hotels here are pretty full according to coach so there must be a lot of people going to the Games at the same time as we are. I thought they would just about have all got there by now.

So you will take a video for me to keep of the Earth as you see it as you rise. You know. Take a few seconds every hour or so if you are not sleeping. I will probably be asleep so you can send it to me when you get to Space City.

Will do. I had better say goodnight as coach is going to have a fit if I don't get a good night's sleep.

Goodnight!

Goodnight!

CHAPTER 10

Hiding a Microchip

Stick it in the roo! ordered Mike.

Where? asked Harry.

Any bloody where. Its bloodwell dead. Exclaimed Mike.

Now what? asked Harry.

Burn the bloody thing. We have to leave only ashes. They won't check that it is only kangaroo ashes and not human ashes.

Harry and Mike were a couple of kilometres up a track in the Alpine National Park. It was winter so they could light a fire without upsetting anyone. Particularly the fire drones that would be buzzing overhead if it was summertime.

They had brought a chain saw in case they did not find enough small wood but it did not look like they would be using it as there was a lot of wood around the place.

Both of them had spent a lot of time in the bush hunting deer, kangaroos, wombats or rabbits or just going for a hike.

They lived nearby in the city of Albury Wodonga. Their families were there but none of them knew of their support for the Freedom groups.

The fire burnt well because the weather was dry and it was not long before there was a pile of ash they could collect and place in an urn labelled Susan. The microchip tracker that had been removed from the real live Susan would now reside at the crematorium until they spread the ashes from a drone over the forest as that is what Susan would have liked if she had lived. That was the story for the robocops anyway.

They had picked up the kangaroo's corpse from the side of the road earlier in the week when they knew they had to do something with Susan's microchip.

When is Tony picking her up? asked Harry.

He should be down tonight. They are coming down for supplies. Said Mike.

So this gives him what? Three women?

Yes, three. Gets them to have a kid each.

So he really isn't upsetting the Government kid to adult ratio?

No, but would you like to try to explain that to any authority if you were him?

Don't they all get a bit lonely just the four of them out in the bush?

They are not the only ones wanting to do their own thing. They meet other groups.

They don't use phones because they can be detected so how does he contact the other groups?

They send drones up high enough for a laser signal to be flashed below them to make other groups aware they want to talk. Then they use lasers.

I think keeping the Earth at about two billion people is a good idea. I suppose Tony agrees with that but why not just have one wife?

He has a high opinion of his genes. He wants to have a lot of little Tonys running around; or Tonies.

It does not worry him that if they catch him they will remove all of his baby making apparatus?

He probably thinks he is well advanced on his gene spreading saga. He has been doing this for a while. He keeps every one of his women very happy. They are all keen on this living with nature idea. With no one complaining and loads of money rolling in from his online businesses run by all his friends he keeps under the radar so to speak.

And the robot cops don't see him in the forest?

He has accommodations which are not detectable by the robocops flying overhead, and people are always out in the forest hunting or whatever. He keeps a couple of people with microchips not removed on hand to show the robocops if they want to see a body.

I still think he is asking for trouble.

Yes, it is a bit different to two parents and two kids, all visible from their microchips. It would worry me that one of these days a robot will actually look at the forest to see what is there rather than just relying on the microchip detector.

I would like to meet this Tony if we can be sure we would not be gathered up with him by the robocops if they do find him and all of us called criminals and given the option of being hunted or just straight out harvested.

I can't say I like the idea of being called a criminal. Pretty poor prospects for criminals. The possibility of winning a hunt or giving up and becoming food for someone's dog makes me hope Tony keeps hidden.

So why are we helping him if the future as a criminal is so poor. And removing microchips is a criminal activity.

Well it is a question of freedom. You and I don't have any. We have our microchips and so the robocops can see where we are at any time and look up our history to see where we have been over the last month or longer. All babies are microchipped at birth but that does not make it right. It is a question of whether having Big Brother knowing all is good. I don't think so but the only thing I can do about it is help Tony.

And the only thing I can do about it is help you. Freedom is something society has decided we cannot afford. London under water shows what freedom does I guess.

When we see him tonight we can ask Tony about a visit. He might not agree though. Our microchips are a health hazard to people like Tony.

CHAPTER 11

Spaceships Alex drinks too much at a Celebration of Life

Well, Jason, he got a bit carried away.

Just can't hold his drink, Thomas. When you get to sixty you would expect a person to know their limits.

Not Alex. Never did remember next day what he said. Always telling others what he thought of them.

It's OK if you are just listening.

Yeah. Entertaining if you are.

What about his thoughts on waiting for Maxwells 2 to 10 to get to their homes.

Well, he has a point. Eight thousand years before Maxwell 10 gets there after it leaves. Who is going to even remember it went.

Just as well they send us a message each year. From 10 we will have eight thousand messages.

Yeah. With the last message getting here forty years after it was sent.

One thing about it. It gives us humans something to do. You don't have a robot that can respond to any emergency and fix it.

Emergency! Being told twenty years after it took place you don't call an emergency.

Well, it could be worse. What about the next phase? Having a spaceship going to Maxwell 14 will mean getting messages several hundred years after they were sent.

Yeah. And there will be tens of thousands of messages.

Too bad that "worm hole" idea wasn't true to speed things up.

True. But if a spaceship could get in one and head off to Maxwell 10 and get there in a few hours instead of eight thousand years would also mean you could have a planet appearing in your bedroom when it came down a worm hole.

Well. Just as well they don't exist.

His comment on the expense was his main point. From the start in 3415 a spaceship every hundred years has been a big expense even with the break.

Humans are unique. No one has yet detected any other life so we need to export us. The Maxwell Empire will have us everywhere.

Now the Milky Way galaxy is one hundred thousand light years across. We need better engines for our spaceships to even get across it in millions of years.

If we want to get to the other galaxies it is going to take a ridiculous amount of time even if we could travel at the speed of light. Just as well they are going to have billions of years to spread to all of them.

Well, Earth will be cooked in a few billion years so I guess humans need to have set up camp elsewhere for them to survive.

So what are these guys talking about?

The Maxwell Government set up a program to spread through space back in the thirtieth century which is called the Maxwell Empire. Ten spaceships are to be built and sent off to planets which can support life as we know it. They are from four or so light years to forty light years away so the time for a spaceship to get to them will vary from eight hundred years for the nearest to eight thousand years for the furthest.

The spaceships are just huge robots taking the DNA message of all living things on Earth to begin again on ten planets.

Maxwell 01 left in 3415 with Maxwell 02 to 05 leaving every hundred years and then a break of five hundred years because they realised they needed to hear from Maxwell 01 whether the procedures used on arrival at the planet worked.

They are built at the factories at Space City.

TABLE OF MAXWELL 01 TO 10

Year left Earth	Planet	Light years away	Travel time in years	First signal from planet
3415	Maxwell 01	4.2	800	4300
3515	Maxwell 02	11	2100	5700
3615	Maxwell 03	12	2300	6000
3715	Maxwell 04	13	2500	6300
3815	Maxwell 05	14	2700	6600
4315	Maxwell 06	16	3100	7500
4415	Maxwell 07	23	4400	8900
4515	Maxwell 08	30	5700	10300
4615	Maxwell 09	39	7400	12100
4715	Maxwell 10	40	7600	12400

Year on Earth first signal received from spaceship in orbit around planet = Year left Earth + Travel time in years + Distance in light years

CHAPTER 12

Space City Factory Visit 2

Scott and Simon are in the bus on the next leg of their Space City tour. Space City's dimensions are impressive.

It is two hundred and fifty thousand kilometres long, consisting potentially of ten thousand twenty five kilometre long rotating segments which give the effect of gravity for people on the wall.

Each segment is ten kilometres in diameter with many still being built and many segment spaces occupied by factories making products for use on Earth or in space.

The space between segments is usually occupied by nonrotating areas suitable for viewing the Earth.

While their next stop is primarily to see the manufacture of communication fibre they will also see the operation of a vertical farm that feeds the millions in Space City.

They intend looking at the Earth from five different locations.

These will be above Indonesia at 130E, India at 90E, Africa at 20E, the Americas at 90W and the Pacific Ocean at 180W.

Their stops are about fifty thousand kilometres apart which their bus will cover in about five hours.

Space City has magnetic acceleration tracks at intervals for getting buses to move at appropriate speeds for travel around Space City.

The tracks are powered by solar energy supplied from solar panels attached to Space City. These also supply the energy to Space City.

Different acceleration tracks have different lengths to get buses which are travelling further to move faster.

When approaching their destination the buses have hydrogen fuelled rockets to slow down.

Scott and Simon are in a high speed bus on their way to their next stop.

CHAPTER 13

The hunt and Dad and Davey

Wake up, Davey. The hunt has got to a promising point.
Dad, how long has it been going.

About an hour. They have had the brains to go in all directions and so far no one has been caught but that is about to change I think. It is why I woke you up.

So we are in Lagos, Nigeria. It must be a bit hot.

Yes, they are in a jungle area south of what is now under water.

So now Lagos no longer has Victoria Island. There is just an inlet from the Atlantic Ocean.

Yes, the huge body of water that separated Lagos from the mainland is now just part of the ocean.

The baddies could be hiding in the water.

If they had enough oxygen they could last long enough to be free but the hunters are dragging listening devices over the water to hear them if they are there. Then they are going to blow them up.

You mean literally blow them up. With a bomb?

Yes. It was expected someone would go swimming.

BOOM

Well, that was quick. No sooner had you told me what could happen and it did. Can you see a body?

Two. They might not have been close together. That was a big explosion.

They must have been scared of snakes.

Possibly. The local snakes would be good and poisonous.

The video guy must be up in the air. I hope he is playing by the rules and not letting the hunters know where the other two are.

Speaking of snakes. Well, crocodiles. That one is not huge but it could take a chunk out of you.

Is it dead or just asleep?

Snoozing. Just waiting for someone running from the hunters to step on it; then chomp.

With four hunters now for each baddie it should not take long now. I need to go back to bed soon.

Have something to eat. A hunt is not a hunt without enjoying some good food while you watch.

You sure have got lots of stuff for us to eat. You must have thought it was going to take a long time before they were killed.

Look! He is jumping all over the place. A snake is hanging on to his arm. It is all black. A reptile to the rescue.

I guess we now only have one to go.

You would think someone would put him out of his misery and shoot him. Right. They were obviously listening. Now definitely just one to go.

The video guy has him. He is up a tree. Right up the tree. The hunters can't see him.

The dog can smell him though. Go Fido.

All eight of them are using him for target practice. He is falling out of the tree.

Well. I thought that would last much longer. I will put the food away. You can go back to bed. Goodnight Davey.

Goodnight again Dad. Thanks for waking me up.

CHAPTER 14

Bus to Moon City 3

Hi Kailee. Did you see the video?

Yes Jimmy. I am just so jealous. That view as you rise up the Space Elevator is just so great.

Yes, it is. But I also managed to do some study. We have enough room in the pod to eat, sleep and work. Have you done the exercises on Rising Sea Levels for Stage 9E?

Yes, I like Earth Science. It must have been a really bad time for people living near the sea when it first started.

And to think it is caused by them burning all the coal and oil and not keeping it for us to use. And the air still has too much carbon dioxide in it so sea levels are still rising. They are now at twenty metres

And it will be going to sixty metres. Sixty metres! Can you believe it? Melbourne under water. And Perth. I had ancestors who lived in Perth but all their houses will be under water in the future if they aren't already. Complained Kailee.

I wish they had stopped burning coal. There are so many cities that we will never see because they were covered in water. Like London. And Dublin. And Limerick. My convict ancestors came from places that are now all under water.

About the only good thing was that with the trench the robots dug Lake Eyre became huge and became a sea inside Australia. So now we have Eyre Sea.

I will have to go Kailee. We are going to a restaurant for dinner. Then we have a tour of Space City before we come back to our hotel to sleep. Then tomorrow we take the bus to the Moon. I don't think I will be able to call you until I get to the Moon. I'm told calling from the Moon bus is very expensive. Bye Bye.

Bye, Jimmy. I look forward to hearing about Space City.

Jimmy left his room to join the others. Not that it was really a room. More like a large cat box like he had for Bobbie, his cat. Really just a bit longer and a bit wider than Bobbie's cat box. If he wanted to do any study while he was in Space City he could because he could do all that he wanted on his phone. He had earplugs so he did not disturb anyone else and he had several podcasts on his history subject that he had to listen to, and videos he needed to watch before he returned to Earth. These were on maths, physics, chemistry and geography. He also had to record a hologram of his time on the tour, but that would need to be when they were on the Moon. He could leave it until he returned to Earth but everyone said it was better to record your life as you lived it. Then your Life Record was as interesting as possible and your descendants would enjoy watching you.

CHAPTER 15

Celebration of Life Uncle Malcolm is leaving

Dad, Uncle Malcolm doesn't remember any of the people here. No, Davey. Not even me and you.

But we love him. I am really unhappy that his mind has gone.

Yes, with his brain not working it is no longer Uncle Malcolm we talk to.

Lots of people remember him, even if he does not remember them.

Yes, a good turn out for a Celebration of Life.

When are you going to run his hologram.

Soon. It is not too complete. Uncle Malcolm did not update it very often.

So we won't have it walking around talking or singing for the rest of the day. Uncle Malcolm is, or was, a good singer.

Yes, a really good voice. Now of course, he can't remember the words.

So people used to think he would be joining Aunty Joan.

Yes, people used to think there was a heaven they went to when they died. And a hell for baddies.

They thought there was a God who created everything and people worshipped Him. But now people don't think there is a God.

Well, you have a god. Me. Your Grumpy Old Dad. So I'm your GOD.

Yes, definitely grumpy sometimes.

Don't get cheeky Davey. Go and find me a couple of sausage rolls with real meat in them.

What about Rusty. Does he want a sausage roll?

He would love a sausage roll. Get a plateful. He and I will share them.

Here is the food. Grand dad is here.

After he has said hello to Uncle Malcolm bring him over here. He can help me and Rusty eat these sausage rolls.

Davey greets his Grand dad and takes him over to be with his dad. Davey's dad greeted his father.

Hi, Dad. How are you sleeping these days?

Better now, son. I just needed to get out and have a bit of exercise.

So are you making sure we have a good hologram for your Life Celebration?

Well, we've got a whole lot of stuff on the computer, but I don't expect to need a good hologram for a lot of years yet. I guess you are sorry Uncle Malcolm did not keep his up to date all the time.

I'm going to miss him, Dad, and it would have been really good if we could have had him around the place when we wanted to see and hear him.

Me too, son. I will make sure I am up to date with my hologram. Not much has happened this year so far. I did get it up to date at Christmas.

Make sure you include the last Christmas lunch? You just have to have your talk about our family history as part of it.

I forgot. That is on the computer. I will add it tomorrow.

It is going to be like on Mum's birthday. Each year we watch her for an hour or so and we want to be able to do the same with you so you need to keep it up to date; not that I think you are anywhere near your Life Celebration, even if the Life Office says you might be with the testing they do each year.

No problem. Now what is there to drink that goes with a sausage roll?

CHAPTER 16

Hunt at 34

Here it is, Crossbows and Axes, May 23rd, 4576, starting at 2 am GMT, which means 11 am in Albury, Australia, exclaimed Sandy.

Will we stay up to watch it or record it? said Bill.

Stay up, please, said Sandy. It is always more exciting to see the action live.

Well, do you want to set the alarm for 1.45 and try to get some sleep because the last one lasted three and a half hours before they killed them all.

I don't think this one will last that long, do you?

Look, he's not too old. Just thirty one, and he is a fitness fanatic according to the promotion. So it could take even longer for him to be killed or to kill some of them; how many does he have after him anyway?

Goodness, he must be good. They have put eight against him. And they are all young and fit by the look of it. Oh, one is getting on. He must be wanting to go out with a bang instead of just being put to sleep.

Look at those women. I don't think any of them will run out of puff and they all look like fitness types.

Well, do I set the alarm?

Yes, and make sure you wake me up, please.

RING RING RING

Bill and Sandy got out of bed and made a hot drink to sip as they watched the latest hunt.

The hunted, a man called Justin Davies, had been promoting the idea that South America should have its own government rather than be part of the World Government.

His family had all supported him and they were all supposed to have been fish fooded a week ago except Justin had claimed Hunthood and it had taken until now to choose the hunt team and take everyone to Hunt Location 34, which was a good time zone for Asia but not for people like Bill and Sandy, who lived in Birmingham which was now the commercial centre of England as London was going beneath the water.

The sea level should drop when the ice stopped melting at the poles but the carbon dioxide was taking longer than expected to reduce in the atmosphere and the sea level was increasing.

CHAPTER 17

A long lecture from Simon

So how can they get to Maxwell 10 quicker? Asked Scott.

Well, said Simon, the present system is that they leave Earth and accelerate for five years with their fusion drive using up about fifteen hundred tonnes of water to propel the spaceship to get to a speed of about 1,600,000 m/s, that is about 1,600 km/s. This speed they do until the last five years or so and during the time between the spaceship reverses its direction so the engines are now pointing at the way the spaceship is moving. Now when the spaceship fires up its engines they act as a brake and the spaceship starts to slow down. Again it has about fifteen hundred tonnes of water to use but it won't need that much because it weighs less. The spaceship itself weighs six thousand tonnes. The total water at the start of the journey was three thousand tonnes. Half that has been used up. So now the mass is seven and a half thousand tonnes and getting less by the minute. But if the spaceship does not have enough water it does not slow down enough to go into orbit around the planet it is heading for so some allowance is made for a bit of a loss of water. Not slowing down enough means it just goes on forever.

At present the water is taken from the Earth's oceans which because the sea level is rising is helping a very little bit but obviously it will be more efficient to get water from the Moon or asteroids or whatever because less energy will be needed to get the water to Space City.

Answering your question, more engines would mean an increase in the acceleration from 0.01 m/s/s but that would mean needing more water. There could be a system of water carriers travelling with the spaceship for a year or two then giving all the water they have to the spaceship except for enough to come to a stop, reverse direction, go back to Earth and slow down to go back to Space City. Because they would weigh enormously less after they had given the spaceship most of their water it would not take much to slow them down and head back and go into orbit around Earth. No doubt they are still thinking about that but because the robots can just go to sleep and last for thousands of years it is a complication no one thinks is necessary. Our Sun should last for a few billion years so there is no urgency in creating the Maxwell Empire.

Anyway, you know all this. It is in the Stage 12A Input. Dig around in your head. They put it all in there. You just need to find where it is. Or watch out. They will think your brain has packed it in and give you a Celebration of Life and fishfood you.

I remember, exclaimed Scott, I remember. It was just good letting you go on, and on, and on. Anyway, it is time I had a nap. Wake me up if there is anything interesting to see on Earth.

CHAPTER 18

Attempted rescue

Simon, wake up, cried Scott, you will not believe what is going on.

What's that? Scott. The world blowing up?

Just about, a war is going on at 34.

What ridiculous timing. We just left that area. We are nearly to India. But who is having a war?

Lots of people are trying to rescue Justin Davies. It is all over the news.

Why don't the hunters just shoot them all? That sort of thing just does not happen.

They are shooting heaps of them. The video drones are all over the place and are showing dead everywhere.

There were only eight hunters. How are they getting on? Asked Simon, moving so he could see the video image.

There were eight. All the hunters that can get there are joining in. For them it is Christmas. But there are an awful lot of attackers. And they have arms. They are not as good at this sort of thing as the hunters but some hunters have died.

Look at that. There are swarms of baddies. How can there be so many.

Good question. Things like this do not happen.

And on the Moon Bus a call is received by Jimmy.

Jimmy, have you seen the news. Justin Davies has a mob trying to get him away from 34.

Yes, we are all watching it. I was about to call you to see if you were watching. Can you believe this is happening?

Not at all. I am going to hang up. I just wanted to make sure you were seeing this. It just doesn't happen.

Thanks Kailee. I'm glad you did. Bye.

And in Birmingham Sandy and Bill are watching.

Would you believe they could have so many video drones up there so quickly? There are so many it must be a headache for the producer to decide which one is showing the most exciting action.

They are all showing exciting action. People charging around everywhere trying to either rescue Justin Davies or kill the rescuers.

And a lot of those rescuers are trying to kill the hunters. The hunters thought Justin Davies was going to be hard to kill but they did not expect this. No one expected this. It is not what happens.

Well, I'm glad we were waiting to see the action. This is the best action we have ever seen.

Yes, and that is why all the world is watching. Look at those figures. There can't be many people in the world not watching.

This sort of thing just does not happen. No wonder we have company watching 34.

And Davey has a question for his dad.

Dad, can we get the TV from the kitchen to bring in here as well? And the one from your bedroom. And the one from my bedroom. With all these video drones we must be missing some of the action we will never see again.

Good idea, Davey. Get yours and I will get the others so we can watch four at once.

This is exciting. I will remember this forever.

And there is a worried conversation going on between Mike and Harry.

I hope Tony keeps his head down, Harry.

He had better Mike, or we might have a problem too.

Look at all those bodies. None of them had chips. The Government is going to be really checking up on any chipless humans.

That's for sure. Before it was just a case of a few people like Tony who did not like being in the same box as everyone else, but these crazies are well outside the box. Or they were before they decided to all get killed.

Hunters love to hunt. What did they expect the hunters to do? Run away. It just gave them the opportunity to blast away at more than the one or two they normally have a chance to kill.

The Government is going to be finding out how they got to 34 without being noticed. Just make sure Tony does not do anything to get spotted by robocops. With such a big group he is going to be very obvious if they stop relying on just chips to see people.

I'll try. We certainly won't be doing anything for him for a while.

CHAPTER 19

So where did they come from

Well, they have killed them all, said Kevin. Now we can go to bed.

But where did they all come from? Asked Julie.

I guess they were from South America, Justin was causing trouble down there.

Yes, he had the idea that it should govern itself.

Well, we have all had History Inputs to know that is not the way to have everyone happy.

Remember what we got from History Input 9E. The twenty first century. China was intent on convincing nearby countries to side with them.

Lots objected. There was a lot of conflict.

It was lucky the Impact stopped all that.

Bad for the world one way, good in another.

What the Chinese wanted is basically what we have now.

Except that we don't all have to speak Chinese.

Yes, evidently they did make a point of trying to get everyone to do that.

Anyway with translators it doesn't matter anyway.

And it is time for bed. Night.

Night, honey.

CHAPTER 20

Chapter 20 Processing the dead

Hello Kailee. We have been given a few extra minutes because such things just do not happen.

Well, I'm glad you're calling me, answered Kailee. I keep wondering about all those bodies we saw by the time it had all finished. What will they do with them?

In Biology Stage 10A we went to school for an excursion to an animal processing factory. It was compulsory. You will have to go on one when you do that Stage. Said Jimmy.

I am not looking forward to seeing humans cut up. Answered Kailee.

That doesn't happen. Humans are just debrained and then the robots take them to the fish fooder for processing.

So who debrains them?

That has to be a human. Robots aren't allowed to kill an animal. You know that.

Well, that is why they have so many hunters. They can kill any animal.

Yes, that is why so many of them charged off to southern Australia to be part of the battle over Justin Davies.

That is one name that will remain part of history forever.

What a way to be remembered. Responsible for thousands of deaths.

And not all human. In that area there were deer, kangaroos, even koalas and wombats that got killed.

They had so many deaths they had to put huge numbers in the freezers before they could process them. They just were not used to having so many bodies to deal with.

We've both had History Stage 9C. Doesn't it all remind you of the scenes from the wars they had in that century, the twentieth century?

Thank Maxwell we don't have such things going on anymore. How millions could die because one mob is shooting at another mob for years. Having a World Government rather than hundreds of them has been a huge advantage.

I still haven't had Stage 9D. History is not my best subject.

Well, I'm out of time. I'll call you from the Moon. Bye Kailee.

Bye Jimmy

MAXWELL EMPIRE

BOOK 2

TABLE OF CONTENTS

CHAPTER 1

Rusty's dinner

Dad, I don't want to give Rusty his dinner any more.

Why not, Davey?

I could be feeding him Uncle Malcolm and I don't want to.

Davey, the chances of there being any Uncle Malcolm in the tin is really very, very small.

Well, I don't care how small it is I could still be feeding Rusty Uncle Malcolm.

Can you imagine just how small it would be with all those who died trying to free Justin Davies being added to the pet food pile? If you like you can give him chicken until you are sure Uncle Malcolm is all gone.

You pointing out all the dead from 34 are waiting to be processed makes me wonder if he will ever be all gone.

I'm sure he will. But just as well that Rusty likes chicken.

Right, chicken it is. Here Rusty, come and get your dinner.

The Justin Davies people that were not killed are putting on a show at the Arena. Several shows actually. There are so many of them waiting to be fish fooded.

I don't know that I want to watch the June Arena Show. They are usually gruesome but this one is likely to be extremely so; they will want to scare everyone off the idea of rebelling.

Probably a good idea, Davey. I don't know if they will be chased around the Arena by pigs or dogs or something new. There was a suggestion a large number of Hunters wanted to chop off a whole lot of heads, legs, arms and whatever else. They are pretty upset by the number of Hunters killed at Hunt 34 when they tried to rescue Justin Davies.

The Hunters might find they are the hunted. The pictures I have seen of the South Americans shows that they are big and fit and they will be wanting a fight.

Yes, apart from you and a whole lot of other kids not watching I think the audience for this Arena Show will be one of the largest ever. The action is likely to be really exciting with lots of blood and gore.

So there will be even more food to add to the pile with Uncle Malcolm in it. I don't think he will ever disappear.

One thing about it though Davey, it does make you think of my brother every time you go to feed Rusty.

I will think of him for the rest of my life when I go to feed my pets from Rusty One to Rusty Two to Rusty Three. Perhaps there might be a Rusty Four.

People do clone their pets so they have the same looking dog or cat or whatever forever.

No, Dad. I was just thinking they would all have the name Rusty. They would be Dog One then Dog Two and so on. I guess there might even be a cat in there somewhere.

Right, Davey. Just normal dogs or cats.

You could watch the Show with Grandpa, Dad.

Good idea. Your Grandpa and I could make a party of it. Anyway Davey. Seeing Rusty has eaten we had better eat.

Right Dad. I'll let robocook know we are ready to eat.

CHAPTER 2

On the way

If someone was trying to save Justin Davies where do you go on Earth when it is all governed by the World Government? Asked Scott.

Well, said Simon, I guess they had the idea that all South America would join in to help them and it would be the end of just one government.

They were a bit hopeful. The last thousand years has been something few people would like to change from.

Yes, enough freedom to have your own country and own government and own choice to go to war on your neighbours.

Each country needed an army, navy and the rest. The money spent on warfare was tremendous.

The communists used to have the interests of the State being more important than individual freedom. And they had the resources of all the country to use for war.

Like China in the twenty first century.

Yes, thinking about going to war with the USA. Trade wars by the USA started it.

And no wonder. Talk about a rigged system. It is interesting to think what would have happened to the world if there had not been the Impact.

That is relevant to today. Were the Chinese people going to eventually want more freedom? Like Justin Davies and his friends.

Well, they would have had trouble doing a better job of objecting to not having freedom than the NRA in the USA after 2645. Talk about going to war.

Yes, the twenty seventh century had so many conflicts with people objecting to the World Government. A very good time to be a small arms salesman.

Definitely an illegal occupation after the World Government began.

But lucrative enough to get a lot of people involved.

Yes, a bit like the USA when they banned alcohol in the twentieth century, and then drugs. If people want to destroy their bodies it needs to be regarded as their choice and society does not need to regard it as their job to keep the body functioning.

Supplying banned substances was extremely lucrative for criminals. It was better to allow people to do what they wanted. It made drink or drugs much cheaper so criminals lost their income.

The change in attitude of society meant people could do what they wanted with the substances but took responsibility for destroying their bodies or brains.

The idea that humans need to be kept alive no matter how non-human they are had to change.

Religions had to lose control of what society thought. Regarding humans as just another animal was necessary.

Having bodies regarded as a source of protein for other organisms whether the body is a fish or a horse or a human was necessary.

Yes, if a fish couldn't swim or a horse couldn't gallop or a human couldn't think meant fish fooding.

It meant a big change with many people getting very upset by the change and doing things which got them fish fooded for their conduct.

A lot of people being fish fooded was good for the planet because there were still too many people. It had to get down to two billion.

Criminals had a problem with everyone being microchipped by the World Government. Saying you were not in a person's house when they were robbed could be shown to be a lie from the record of your movements which showed you were. Crime was not a good occupation.

Not if you did not want to be fish fooded. With everyone getting their money each month crime was a bit pointless.

I guess some people are just built that way. They like the thrill of being bad.

And then having the long thrill before they are fish fooded.

I wonder if that was what motivated Justin Davies mob. Wanting a life with more excitement from going to war.

Yes, not just losing your microchip but actively working against what the rest of the world regarded as how the Earth should be run.

Perhaps they were just bored.

Well, they should have known they had no chance of success.

So, bored and not interested in putting their names down for any of the other non-boring activities such as spending time on Space City or the Moon or hunting pigs or camels or horses or whichever animal has begun to exceed its appropriate numbers just like humans did.

Some people just do not want to fit in. Too bad it means being fish fooded.

Just as well we want to fit in. I'm going to have a snooze before we get there.

Good idea. Me too.

CHAPTER 3

Kevin and Julie going to London

Hurry up Kevin, the train leaves at 8.30.

I am Julie, this breakfast is just a bit tastier than the usual.

Well, it's not every day we go to London. But if you don't get a move on we won't be.

No problem. Just give me a minute in the bathroom.

Just hurry up. I really want to see the robots at work removing Queen Elizabeth, Darwin, Newton and everyone else from Westminster Abbey and bringing them up here to Birmingham.

Right! Done! Me too! And of course every brick and tile and rebuilding the Abbey up here. Let's get to the station.

We will have a regular tourist attraction with the Houses of Parliament and Westminster Abbey rebuilt here. When the water goes down no doubt they will send them back.

Just when that will be is a problem. The current idea is the water goes up until all the ice melts.

That carbon dioxide is proving a real problem to decrease. Growing trees all over the world might be helping but it isn't obvious.

It certainly makes the view from Space City better. All that green. If it is possible I would like to go up there again.

I guess with some people not wanting to go it might be possible.

70

I just find it difficult to believe that there are people who do not want to see the Earth from outer space. It is just so beautiful.

Yes, even with so much of it covered in water.

Possibly because so much is under water. It would not have been such a good idea to cover all land with trees if the water had not been going up.

They had better hurry up and help. Otherwise people will start cutting them down and adding carbon dioxide to the air.

Yes, I do like a BBQ.

Just as well all the work these days is done by robots. It all would have cost a fortune with humans doing the work.

Yes, having to pay wages to human workers who only work a third of the day for a few days each week doesn't compare with robots that work all day every day for a dose of electricity and no pay.

It pays to be a human in the forty sixth century.

Thank Maxwell there are only two billion humans. I do like having birds around. Just imagine if it was back to fifteen billion.

Or more. Standing room only. I like runaway asteroids.

As long as they hit somewhere else when needed.

Next time perhaps it should hit South America. Justin Davies buddies friends if many more are left need to join the ones caught so far and be squashed.

Well, not so much squashed as squished. It's just as well there have been a few hundred caught. It means there are a couple of dozen for each arena. The Romans had the right idea for entertainment.

Yes, they used lions on Christians to entertain the mob and now we do the same thing but with pigs chasing rebels.

It is a case of a porker getting his own back. Instead of us eating pigs it is pigs eating us, well the bad us.

Anyway Kevin, look up there. The train is nearly here. Just as well you did not eat any more.

Just good timing Julie. London here we come.

CHAPTER 4

Fish fooding bad animals

mum, I have to explain why the third part of the Octet is good.

Well Sammy, what do you think?

I think that if an animal does something really bad it should be fish fooded.

Don't you think that agrees with Octet three?

Yes, so it is that simple.

In the years before the twenties that is what happened, but then in the twentieth century and the rest of the twenties religions thought humans were too precious to be fish fooded, even when they had done really bad things.

We have seen some of the videos and read some of the stories from those times. People were not sensible.

No, if an animal goes around deliberately killing more than one other animal they have to be fish fooded. It will rarely be the case that the action is reasonable.

One video showed a man with guns deliberately killing fifty people in New Zealand. Fifty people. And then they put him in jail. He was young and they spent a fortune keeping him alive until he died of old age, but they should have fish fooded him immediately.

If you look at the world population back then there were over seven billion humans. Much too many. Other animals were becoming extinct because of the number of humans. And then they refused to fish food baddies like that.

Religions would not let women have control of their bodies. When a woman was not wanting a baby she did not want religions said that what she wanted was not significant, she had to have it. There are so many things wrong with that idea.

It is because of religions that the man in New Zealand was not fish fooded. Having a belief that humans are something really special and are not on the same level as other animals gives society a warped view of life. If you accept all animals are equal you have a better view of life.

Mum, have you had a baby you did not want so you had to abort it?

Yes, Sammy. Before we had you we had to abort a baby. We did not know I was pregnant. It was soon after we got married. Your dad and I went for a week's holiday in Space City. Unfortunately a solar flare happened that week. We were in a part of Space City not protected because we were looking at the view of the Earth. It meant the baby was not normal. Later on you came along.

So in the twenties you would have had to keep the baby?

In some places. Some places were not so religious. Religion can be a problem for people. It is why people now have the Octet. You have to remember that back in the twenties things were a lot different.

Yes, people had to work. Robots did not do all the work.

Do remember that if you want to work you can. There are lots of jobs for people who like to work. But not only work. Some places did not have ways to allow women to not have babies. Some women had a dozen or more.

So when they got to twelve babies they could not say they did want any more.

It wasn't allowed. And then there was the problem with many places of people being extremely poor. It was not like now with every person having an income whether they work or not. Some people then could not find a job. They had no money. They had a dozen children. But they could not say "Enough!"

I have got off the topic of Octet three.

Remember what it says. "This life is all you are going to have so value it. Do not cause society to remove your life from you because of your conduct." People need to value their lives to be able to follow Octet three. And they need to regard the lives of others as valuable so they do not harm them.

In the past people were in charge of vehicles on the roads. They could drive vehicles they were not authorised to and at speeds well above speed limits, and dangerously.

That sort of thing cannot happen today of course as vehicles are all robots taking us where we want to go but in the past it could be dangerous if other drivers were not thinking our lives were valuable.

I have read so many stories of people driving vehicles and causing the deaths of other people and then being punished very little.

Society surely had a peculiar attitude towards drivers who caused accidents. Possibly because they felt they might have been in that situation themselves if they were not being attentive enough at the time. Remember the story from our ancestor where his car had been hit in the back, and in the front, and on one side, at different times by other drivers, and none of the times was his fault.

But if a person drove a car without permission, and then drove dangerously, without regarding other road users and their lives as important, I think if that person caused another person's death they should be fish fooded.

Yes, and you will no doubt have read of a huge number of examples of twenties people behaving like that before all vehicles became robots and were no longer dependent on humans for their behaviour on the road.

So if the Octet had been implemented in the twenties the roads would have been safer because all those drivers would have been off the roads because they were fish fooded.

Yes, so these days it is so much safer to be on the roads because the robots do not misbehave like some humans did. Of course there can be a problem when a person deliberately confuses a robot vehicle and causes an accident.

Yes, and then I think Octet three means the person doing the confusing must be automatically fish fooded even if there is no accident or damage because there is the potential for enormous damage because of the speeds the robot vehicles travel at.

Well, I guess you have discussed that enough to be able to write your report that Octet three is good.

Yes, thanks for your help mum. I'll do that now then I'll have lunch.

Live your life while following the guidelines of THE OCTET. In the forty sixth century religion is no longer a part of human life and all people follow THE OCTET.

THE OCTET

1. Live your life with the knowledge that this time you have alive is all that you are going to get, with no previous life having been had by you or that there will be another life after you die, so value this life.
2. Humans are social animals so enjoy and value time spent together with other animals, particularly those of your species.
3. This life is all you are going to have so value it. Do not cause society to remove your life from you because of your conduct.
4. Look after the well-being of your mind and body.
5. Take full responsibility for your actions.
6. One should treat others as one would like others to treat oneself.
7. All living things have a right to exist and all animals are equal.
8. Value the future on a timescale longer than your own.

CHAPTER 5

Moon City in the Moon

Jimmy has arrived in Moon City. He and the group leave the pod on the Moon Space Elevator.

Some of the group are staying in hotels but others are staying with friends or family members. Jimmy has a friend from his online connections called Ben. During the Moon Bus trip he had a call from Ben who asked him to stay with him and his family in their apartment.

Ben recognises Jimmy from the time they have spent online together.

Jimmy, I'm Ben. Welcome to the Moon.

Well Ben, you look just like your picture, greeted Jimmy.

Jimmy, this is my friend Jenny.

Hi, Jenny. Thanks for meeting me.

So you just have the one bag?

Yes, we were keeping the weight down and I am being loaned any equipment I need while I am here.

Do you want something to eat before we head home?

Good idea. But I will give Kailee a call to let her know I am here.

Right. You can do that as we walk to the food court.

Hi, Kailee. I'm in the Moon. You remember Ben. He has met me at the Moon Bus port. He has got me staying at his place.

That's good Jimmy. You will get to see some of the things you two talk about.

And do some of the things he tells me about.

How was the trip?

It was OK. Not exciting after the Justin Davies hoo haa.

Good. I guess I will let you go. I will talk to you later.

Yes. We are about to eat. Bye.

Bye.

So Ben, I think everyone was watching Hunt 34 and them trying to rescue Justin Davies.

Yes Jimmy, Jenny called me to make sure I watched the action. Mum and Dad stayed up to watch it all as well. Such things just don't happen.

What I don't understand Jimmy, said Jenny, was how so many people got to 34 without anyone knowing.

There is no doubt going to be a big investigation to try to find out how, replied Jimmy. Just now I will investigate your Moon food.

Ben lives on the Moon in Moon City and his Mum got him to invite Jimmy to stay with the family in their apartment because she knew how much time the two had spent online talking to each other.

Ben spends a lot of time with his friend Jenny. He would like it to be a bit more than friend but at present it is friend. Ben has heard a lot about Kailee and is hoping Jimmy thinks about Kailee a lot.

Like Jimmy Ben is a sports person. Because of the low gravity people are advised to get a fair amount of exercise to keep their bones healthy People also go down to Earth regularly.

Ben will be competing with Jimmy in the skiing and also competing in the cycling.

Moon City is in the Moon. It is underground.

There are schools, shops, places to work if you want to and places to play and lots of places to eat the food they like best.

Sometimes the people of Moon City visit the surface, but generally they work and play in this world beneath the surface.

When they do visit the surface they never go on their own, but always with at least one other person, and best of all, a big group of people. While the domes on the surface are rarely punctured it can happen and in such circumstances they think that the more help they have the better the chance of survival.

The Space Elevator terminus is near a large industrial area. Asteroid material from the factories above the Moon is used on the Moon surface as well as being sent to Space City for use over the Earth. The terminus is also the gateway for passengers arriving or departing on the Moon Buses.

After the meal they descend to Ben and Jenny's level.

On exiting the lift Jimmy cannot help but be impressed by the space around him and exclaims.

Well, I've seen the images of down here but in real life it is huge.

Yes, said Ben, because on the Moon people found it better to live under the ground because the surface was a health hazard.

So no one lives on the surface, said Jimmy.

Not at all, answered Ben. Well, that is not quite true. Some places have shielded domes which are safe.

So having no air or magnetic field to reduce the effect of radiation from space makes the surface a health hazard.

Yes, so the first Moon dwellers made big tunnels in the Moon with the rock between them and the surface providing protection from the radiation.

And they are long, said Jimmy. I can see it goes on forever.

Yes, said Ben. The tunnels are very long. The tunnels are so long that it takes weeks to walk along all of them. This means it is good for me for bike riding because I can travel for many kilometres before returning to the same path.

Jenny made a contribution. Humans require oxygen so some tunnels have farms in them. The plants produce both food and oxygen. The humans and other animals produce carbon dioxide. We can take you on a tour of a farm when you two are not competing.

Jimmy could see that this level in Moon City had apartment buildings in it. Shops were under the apartments in most of the buildings they went past.

We had better wave down a tram said Ben, otherwise it will take us ages to get home.

If you want to, said Jenny, we can also take you to see the industries that are underground that are on separate levels to housing. They are generally manned by robots but there will be some humans. Most industries are on the surface because robots do not need air and can work more freely in the open than underground.

Jimmy knows much of this because the Geography Education Input 8 had a section on the Moon and Moon City. He does not cover it all in detail until he does Geography Education Input 11D.

That will be probably in a couple of years as geography is a subject he is progressing in at a normal rate.

At present he is in Stage 9D in Geography but others vary with Earth Science being at Stage 9E and Biology Stage 10B.

From the farm levels the Moon has oxygen from the plants and also it gets oxygen from the electrolysis of water.

Solar cells and fusion reactors give Moon City lots of electricity. While solar cells are a much cheaper source of electricity they do not have the reliability of a fusion reactor.

Earth found this out many years ago when the sun was obliterated in the Northern Hemisphere because an asteroid impacted the Earth and threw a huge amount of material into the atmosphere.

No sunlight meant no electricity for those places reliant on solar cells for electricity.

While the lack of sunlight was experienced for only a matter of months in the north it was remembered as being significantly longer because of its impact on the lives of the people in the Northern Hemisphere directly and as a result of the movement of people from the north to the south the impact on the lives of people in the Southern Hemisphere.

The impact of the Impact was to significantly reduce the number of humans which was a very good outcome for the rest of the living things on Earth. There had been too many humans and the reduction resulted in a movement to make human levels closer to the two billion advocated by many scientists.

In the south the sunlight was not affected.

The harnessing of fusion reactors once they had been developed on Earth had meant an unending supply of electricity for very little cost because the deuterium necessary to fuel them composed one ten thousandth of the water in the oceans.

This meant that there was fuel available until the Sun would explode in billions of years' time.

Also it was very cheap to extract from the oceans.

The deuterium fuel for the Moon's fusion reactors is obtained from the water they get from the Moon, Earth or the Asteroid Belt.

The cheap and plentiful electricity meant that lighting and warming Moon City was assured.

People can have pets in Moon City but they are controlled by type and size. For example, there are no Rottweiler dogs as they were a big dog and people thought they had a tendency to attack people.

There are cats, fish, terriers, and even frogs.

Some parks for people to enjoy are not flat. They have an undulating landscape which while not hills makes the scenery more interesting especially as they also come with running water in small streams.

All parks have trees. This is why apartments need to have at least 6 levels, as the parks will then be high enough for trees to grow.

Some parks have a continuous slope so they can be permanent ski fields.

The ski field in Ben and Jenny's part of the city is off their level, level 5.

It slopes upwards from its entrance to level 5 at an angle of 20 degrees and is permanently covered in snow.

A ski lift operates 24 hours a day controlled by the Moon City Sports Department staff. Most of the work is done by robots but humans are necessary as they can respond more quickly and appropriately in the case of emergencies.

There are hydrogen fuel cell powered electric cars for hire to travel longer distances and for short distances people walk or ride bicycles or use the robot busses of the public transport.

They got off at Ben's apartment block. His address was at APT 5/035/3/19, York Town, Moon City, Moon. That is Level 5, Building 035, Floor 3, Apartment 19.

Ben's mother greeted them.

You look just like your image. I'm pleased you came, Jimmy.

Thank you for inviting me, Mrs Kimton. It is good to meet you. Are you hungry?

No thanks, we ate at the Food Court.

Right. You three can get better acquainted while I prepare something for dinner then.

Thanks Mum. We'll get Jimmy set up then we might take him shopping if he is up to it.

Don't wear the poor boy out too much. He has just had a long trip to get here.

No problem. We will look after him.

CHAPTER 6

Scott and Simon Viewing Bangladesh

Come on Scott. Let's go to the viewing area.

I really hate being in the zero gravity areas, Simon.

We won't be long. I want to have a good look at Bangladesh.

Right. I want to see what exactly is still above water too.

Both of them put on their boots for walking along the steel path to the viewing area which does not rotate like the section they had been in.

The Observation Area is air filled and warm but they also have to put on their spacesuits as a precaution against something going wrong.

Their magnetic boots have electromagnets on their bottoms to hold them to the steel plated pathways.

The electromagnets in the boots are turned on when their foot is descending and off when their foot is ascending.

They are also attached to a guide rail because there is no gravity in the Observation Area and while they can drift readily along it their attachment stops them drifting out of control throughout the whole area.

Well, it's not all under water.

So ten percent or so still above water is good?

I guess it is pretty bad. Losing ninety percent of your land when you are overcrowded in the beginning makes you wonder where they have all gone.

Well, with the Impact a lot of them headed to Australia. Together with many millions of others of course.

Yes, and that was a long time before the water got up. So I guess the population was not as big as I thought.

As the water rose they would have upset the Indians but by then we had the World Government. And religions were gone.

Yes, the original division was because of different religions. And of course India had also lost a lot of people in the Impact.

I wonder if there were any Bengal tigers left before the Impact.

I hope so. But if there weren't I hope they have stored their DNA. Where they would have been is all under water. Not much hope of getting any DNA now.

With the water still rising a lot of people are still going to have to move. And there will definitely be no tiger home left out of the water.

And only a very small bit of Bangladesh still out of it. There must be a lot of the world's population thankful for it now having just one government and no religions so they can be moved to anywhere safe.

The Burmese would have just moved a bit north if they were still there. All their bottom bit is under water.

I am glad they started storing the DNA of all species in the twenty first century. When the water does go down the Bengal tigers can be reintroduced to their original area.

Yes. Too many humans was one problem. Water going up was another. Let us hope that when the disaster caused by the humans from the beginning of the twenties is over the world will have a sensible government and a sensible number of humans.

That message is made loud and clear to Maxwell 01 and the rest of the new Earths. Let's hope the new humans heed the advice and don't reproduce like rabbits.

Anyway Simon, I have had enough of a look at water, water, everywhere over Bangladesh. Let's return to the comfort of our seats.

Good. I have seen enough too. I would not like to have been a Bangladeshi.

CHAPTER 7

Fred has another homework exercise

um, I have to report on a change in the twenty second century that said that cars must be controlled by robots because cars are lethal weapons.

Yes, well Fred, humans doing the right thing would be all right but the stories from history show us that young people would steal cars, drive them too fast, have accidents and kill people. Adults would do the wrong thing as well and drive while not capable because of drink or drugs. Humans driving cars was usually all right but robot cars are always all right.

It must be really enjoyable to steer a car yourself with the wind in your hair.

Yes, most people did the right thing but it only takes a few doing the wrong thing and killing people to spoil it for everyone.

From those times we have stories of citizens in the United States of America having access to unsuitable firearms and some of them then killing a large number of people because the guns could fire many bullets in a short time.

Yes, the wrong weapons in the wrong hands result in the wrong result. No matter whether it is a gun or a vehicle the result can be the same.

I suppose I could drive a car on a race track.

Yes, that would be a way of driving yourself. It is just not allowed on public roads. Of course if a farmer wants to drive himself on his farm he can.

It began with a computer which made sure the car was being driven correctly by the correct person.

The roads needed sensors so the car computer would know the appropriate speed and then the computer would talk to the driver if the speed was excessive.

You could have the scenario like: Attention Driver, You are exceeding the road speed limit. It is 80 km/h. You are doing 90 km/h. Is there a legitimate reason for this excess speed? No. Then I am reducing the car's speed to 80 km/h. Yes. Then I am contacting the traffic police to expedite our travel to your destination.

Well said, Fred. And what would be the scenario if a thief was attempting to drive the vehicle? It is easy to see that with suitable devices cars can't be driven.

Yes, many deaths on the roads were the result of young drivers speeding in cars they had stolen and driving too fast. The computer would be able to identify the person attempting to start the car as not being authorised to do so.

So what would it say?

It would say something like Hello driver, you are not authorised to use this vehicle. Exit the car immediately. Driver, exit now. Driver. You have not exited. The car will not start. The doors are locked. The police have been called. Any attempt to damage the car will cause a gas to be emitted to make you unconscious.

Well, another good scenario Fred. As we have seen eventually the roads did have the sensors and the cars had computers to ensure vehicles were less like lethal weapons on the roads.

Yes, In Australia in one year in the early 21st century there were 238 deaths from people shooting other people with guns and around the same time there were 1226 deaths on the roads from car crashes. That is, there were five times as many deaths from cars but there was no great clamour to stop cars being owned and driven by any section of the population. They were not sensible.

Young drivers were often the problem. An item I have listened to that was on the Australian Government radio at the time tried to make the rest of the population feel responsible for the dangerous driving of young people.

Having stiff penalties would have been appropriate if there had been any probability that speeding young people would have been caught in the act of inappropriate driving behaviour but if a nonlicensed young driver wanted to drive they would steal a car and go speedily enough so that the police refused to chase them. Bad driving should have resulted in apprehension. To not have the police catch a person behaving dangerously is wrong.

I think they should have had the OCTET and an attitude that a person wilfully endangering others needed to be fishfooded. They used to put people who had been really bad in prison and support them for many years before they were released back into society or they died.

Yes, it was many centuries before people were regarded as animals and treated as a being with responsibilities to the other animals. They thought they were a mortal being made in the image of a mythical figure which meant they were somehow above all other animals.

Many people enjoy going into the forest and hunting with their guns to bring down other animals but they have regard for the well being of the other animals and make sure their death is as painless as possible. Not like some of the stories I have read from the early twenties when people driving vehicles would deliberately run down animals to kill them for fun and leave them to suffer. Fishfooding would be their fate these days.

Hunting is one of the activities I really enjoy doing with dad. We have to be very quiet moving through the forest to get close enough to the deer to make sure it dies immediately when I shoot it. It is good to have the skill it takes.

That reminds me that dinner needs my attention. You can get on with your report.

CHAPTER 8

Grant asks

Dennis, if you were a robot terraforming a planet like Maxwell 01 how many humans would you make in the beginning?

Well, Grant, it would depend on so many variables that it is impossible to say. The robots producing the plants and animals would need to be able to work it out for themselves.

When it came to plants it would not matter how many you made just so long as there were enough of them as food for the animals.

The food plants would need to be varied though to give a balanced diet and protect from some possible diseases. Like men needing broccoli to avoid prostate cancer.

One advantage of having completed Biology Stage 10E for sure.

The story about Captain Cook's voyages and avoiding scurvy is another reason they would need to have grown the right plants for the humans.

Growing a garden of beautiful flowers would not do the health of the humans much good; apart from their mental health anyway. So the robots must know what plants the animals need to have to eat.

Yes, there would not be any point throwing all types of seeds around without consideration of the needs of the new animals.

That is apart from the plants producing oxygen of course.

It must take years to get sufficient plants of the types you want.

You have the DNA and you make cells of those plants using your algae but then you need to grow the seeds, collect more seeds, and keep repeating it all until you have enough seeds.

Now you are remembering what Biology Stage 10D included.

Sorry, I am preaching to the converted so to speak.

The message saying they had got chickens and were about to start humans was hundreds of years after Maxwell 01 got there so it has been a lengthy process.

That brings up the question, what came first, the chicken or the egg.

A new take on an old question. Because the stored DNA was used to change the algae cells to chicken cells it has to be that the chicken was produced first and then it laid eggs.

As long as it was a hen of course.

They would have thought of that.

When the humans start eating solids the robots will have to feed them all the male chickens so the females are kept to make more chickens, and also eggs for the humans.

Bit sexist. But true.

Your still not getting to tell me how many humans you think they have produced, Dennis.

Grant, is it relevant seeing there are so many variables or are you just worried you do not design enough different birthday cards.

That is a thought. We don't know their names. I can't do cards at all. Whether there are ten or ten thousand they are going to get a bit upset to get a card for their third birthday saying NUMBER 56, HAPPY BIRTHDAY, or NUMBER 256, HAPPY BIRTHDAY. Just as well I wasn't thinking about birthday cards.

Still being a bit sexist. Do you think they would have equal numbers of boys and girls?

Good question. If you want to make the most humans quicker you would have a few males and lots of females.

Like having a herd of cows and one bull to service them all.

I wonder what the robots were told.

Just as well Maxwell 01 gets to answer our questions after only an eight year wait. It will be nowhere near as satisfying for our great, great etcetera grandchildren when they want to know what has happened on the other planets.

We could of course ask the robot programmers what the robots were told to do.

Read their notes anyway seeing it left over a thousand years ago.

I had a think about my reason for growing the plants in domes. You know. You asked me why before.

For producing oxygen. Yes I remember.

Well, a lot of the oxygen would come from the breakdown of the water they use for making hydrogen for use in the airships to disperse spores or seeds all over the planet. And the rest would come from the plants.

True. I should have thought that myself.

The air outside the domes has no oxygen so is poisonous to the new animals that the robots make so all the animals are confined to the domes.

So I guess it will give the humans a chance chase a chook or to pick their own apple or strawberry or flower.

If they are confined to going walkabout in the domes they need a big garden. Better than just dirt. And they will need a lot of domes with different designs.

Yes, they can't go walkabout outside the domes so they need a lot of different ones so it gives them a more interesting home.

It is going to be interesting to see just how many humans Maxwell 01 did make.

And what the sex ratio is.

Just as well we are at the beginning of this adventure. It is going to be an interesting lifetime.

True. I can't wait for the next message from Maxwell 01.

Me too. I hope it is soon.

THE BEGINNING OF THE MAXWELL EMPIRE

In the thirtieth century the Maxwell Government set up a program which is called the Development of the Maxwell Empire to spread humans throughout space.

Ten spaceships are to be built initially and sent off to planets which can support life as we know it.

They are from four or so light years to forty light years away so the time for a spaceship to get to them will vary from eight hundred years for the nearest to eight thousand years for the furthest.

The spaceships are just huge robots taking the DNA message of all living things on Earth to begin again on ten planets.

Maxwell 01 left in 3415 with Maxwell 02 to 05 leaving every hundred years and then a break of five hundred years because they realised they needed to hear from Maxwell 01 whether the procedures used on arrival at the planet worked.

They are built at the factories at Space City.

TABLE OF MAXWELL
01 TO 10

Year left Earth	Planet	Light years away	Travel time in years	First signal from planet
3415	Maxwell 01	4.2	800	4300
3515	Maxwell 02	11	2100	5700
3615	Maxwell 03	12	2300	6000
3715	Maxwell 04	13	2500	6300
3815	Maxwell 05	14	2700	6600
4315	Maxwell 06	16	3100	7500
4415	Maxwell 07	23	4400	8900
4515	Maxwell 08	30	5700	10300
4615	Maxwell 09	39	7400	12100
4715	Maxwell 10	40	7600	12400

Year on Earth first signal received from spaceship in orbit around planet = Year left Earth + Travel time in years + Distance in light years

CHAPTER 9

Jimmy goes skiing

A day of rest after the trip to the Moon allows for a visit to a farm.
Wake up Jimmy. We can go for a practice on the ski run.

I'm awake, Ben. Good idea. Is it far?

No, just a way down along our level. Only a few minutes by tram.
Have you got spare skis?

Yes, I borrowed some gear for you when you said you would stay.
I remembered your size. Just so long as it is the same.

It is, but just let me try them on.

Yep. Good fit. How much does it cost?

Nothing. It is run by the city.

Even better. Exercise then eating. I suppose breakfast comes
second.

It surely does. Let's go.

An hour later they are back from their skiing.

That is great Ben, having your ski slope next door so to speak.

Yes, one advantage about making your home by drilling it out
of rock. By keeping it enclosed it makes maintaining the snow less
difficult.

And so many people out there in the early morning. What is it
like later in the day.

Crowded. Even with fields on several levels people like it so much it can be a problem with so many people.

With your low gravity it meant not so much speed. Good for jumps though.

Yes, and some of the other slopes are steeper for more speed, like for the competitions starting tomorrow.

I look forward to it. But for now your start to the day has been one to remember.

Glad to hear it. Now see what you think of a Moon breakfast. Jenny will be here a bit later for the farm visit.

After breakfast I will give Kailee a ring to let her know how it is going.

Jenny turns up after breakfast.

Morning Jenny. Jimmy is making a call to Kailee.

Morning Ben. I will watch the video you made of you two skiing while I wait.

Jimmy makes his call.

Hello Kailee, this is the Moon calling.

Hi Jimmy. This is Earth replying.

Have you watched the video I sent of the two of us skiing?

Yes. So exciting. So many rolls while you were up in the air. And so long up there. Just so different to here. So did you like skiing on the Moon?

It was so different. You don't go as fast but when you do a jump you go up and up and up. Scary at first.

The video showed Ben's skiing was very good?

It shows that practice makes perfect. He was just so good. He did so many rolls when he was in the air. I am going to have a problem in the competitions.

Have the others from Albury been there before?

Some of them. They did say it would be different but I did not expect it to be just so different.

You will have to be a quick learner Jimmy.

True. A very quick learner.

Well, best of luck with your skiing. At least running will not be a problem.

We have just had breakfast. Ben is taking me around Moon City with Jenny.

So how do you get around?

Ben and Jenny like bike riding so we will be doing that but there are trams to hop on or cars to use.

What about going for a run? Is it too crowded?

Not at all. We will be going for a bit of a run. That is me and Ben and his friend Jenny.

So you have been a bit busy even before breakfast. And more so by the end of the day with skiing, sightseeing, bike riding and running.

Yes, I guess. But I need to make good use of my few days here.

I look forward to being busy up there some day.

Get into sport Kailee. It takes you out of the world.

Ha Ha! I will get up to Space City before you get back I hope.

That would be good. We could tour it together.

I am trying to get there. Well mum and dad are. Some people have cancelled their visit and mum and dad say we may be there as you return.

Great! I hope it happens.

Thanks. I hope we get to see bits of Space City together.

Me too. Bye.

Bye.

Jimmy greets Jenny.

Morning Jenny. You can see I need a lot more practice before tomorrow.

Well, for a first effort here on the Moon your skiing was very good. Of course, Ben has been doing it forever.

Ben, after our tour I had better get you to take me down for another session. Will that be okay?

For sure. Let's show you some Moon farming first.

CHAPTER 10

Tony's camp near Dartmouth

I don't get why the robocops are fooled by Tony just having alpacas all over their camp, said Harry.

They don't just have alpacas. They have heaps of deer, kangaroos, wallabies, dogs, cats and whatever else will hang around.

Have you been to the camp?

Yeah. All the homes are underground. Shielded from the infrared detectors and whatever.

How do they get their electricity?

They have solar panels floating on Dartmouth Lake. They produce hydrogen which they pipe to the homes. Hydrogen fuel cells give them electricity whenever they need it.

It seems a lot of trouble just to not be microchipped.

Extreme for sure. I guess if you have it in your head that you don't want to be always under the gaze of Big Robot then you will go underground, literally.

So they have friends who get them the gear they need.

Yeah. Bit of a risk but a lot of people like the idea but are not brave enough to do it themselves. Like us.

True. I like the comfort of a normal lifestyle even if Big Robot knows my every move.

That is why if we do visit him it will be as part of a deer hunt so we will not actually stop walking.

Yes, the Robocops would see from our record of movement that we had stopped for too long.

Of course we could just be having a cup of tea.

I need to get a deer. I supply the family dogs with meat and the supply at home is getting low.

Just as well that we are heading up there in a day or two. I need to get a spare tank of hydrogen for the vehicle.

So the car gets us to Dartmouth. How do we avoid having the vehicle show the robocops it is sitting in one place for a long time?

It will be. But in the middle of Dartmouth. We will row a boat across the lake to near their camp and just keep walking looking for deer, but talking to people.

But we will get a deer. I need dog meat.

For sure. There are lots of deer up there. Just shoot one not on his doorstep because it might be a pet.

We might need a hand to get it back to the vehicle.

We will gut it up there so it will only weigh half as much. Make sure you don't shoot a huge one.

If they live underground Mike, they had to dig out their homes. How did they do that?

Tony got a few construction robots and had them do the whole thing. Those things work day and night so it did not take all that long.

So has he still got them?

Yes. He uses them to chase up gold. It's one of the ways he makes money. The whole area has been a source of gold for centuries. More so back before the twenties but he still finds some.

And he has not come to the attention of the robocops.

Not before the Justin Davies episode. That will make him be more careful.

I hate to think what would be done to them all if they are caught.

We need to be careful. We could have the same fate for helping him.

Just as well we need to get some dog food. We have an excuse for chasing around the countryside.

Let's hope we don't meet any problem people, or non-people.

CHAPTER 11

Alex complains about World Government

One thing about Alex, whispered Jason, a few drinks and he tells the World how it should run things.

It would be all right, said Thomas quietly, if his views could not upset more than a few people.

Come on Alex, we will help you get home. We have all had a good night.

Yes, Alex. Let's go. We have a car waiting.

Jason and Thomas helped their friend who had enjoyed much too much of the free booze at the work celebration out to the car and took him home.

They then sat in the car for a while to discuss their friend's comments.

He has a point about freedom. We don't have any. Not much anyway.

Well, I guess in one way it is better. We don't run the risk of being killed by an invading army.

Yes, in the Twenties there was a lot of that. With a lot of death and destruction.

While Alex was going on before about the cost of the Maxwell Empire program there are huge savings these days from having just one government because we don't need armies, navies, air forces, and space corps, because we aren't hundreds of nations with the possibility of armed conflict between them.

Yes, basically we all follow the Octet.

If we follow that the problem of self-interest is reduced.

In the days when people had to work to make money to live it was different.

Now with a regular payment to cover whatever you need and being included in the lists for activities you are interested in so you do them when you get to the top of the list.

Like when we get to go to Space City. I am well down on the list for that.

With two billion people on the lists and only a million or so going to visit Space City each year it is just as well a lot of people don't like the idea of going into space.

The list for going to the Moon is even more difficult to get to the top of.

It has been the same forever; sports people go everywhere first.

Yes, the competitions going up there at present are being watched by a huge number of viewers.

The low gravity makes for some really spectacular ski jump motions.

It makes me sorry I was not all that keen on sports.

That brings us back to what Alex said. With all of us under constant surveillance because of our microchip the amount of exercise we do is known so when we do not do enough a message comes to do some more.

Yes, talk about a nanny state. It is difficult to have a not so good life style. When they complained about that a couple of millennia ago they had no idea just how bad it could get.

When Big Robot knows how many steps you take each day, how many laps you do in the pool, when you get puffed out, you have no chance of a sedentary life style.

Well, it's good for your health.

It is another aspect of what Alex said. Just no freedom at all.

Actually changing the situation so you do have freedom is definitely a health hazard.

Yes, getting rid of your microchip is possible but the probability of a short life also becomes very possible.

Definitely not a good time for anyone living without a microchip. The Justin Davies crew saw to that.

South America is getting a good look over to find any more of his friends so they can be fish fooded.

Like any good nanny state. Protecting us from our own stupidity.

I guess muttering a tune about wanting to be treated as an adult would be regarded very poorly.

Over the last thousand years or so there must have been a lot of mutterings.

Yes, not being regarded as an individual who could possibly do sensible things without worrying about what Big Robot thought is belittling.

It is not new though. Some countries in the past treated their citizens as adults while others were just as bad nanny states as what we now have.

The trouble is so many people in the past did conduct themselves without concern for their own well being.

Yes, history has so many examples we had better appreciate our lack of freedom.

So much for the Alex topic of the day. Let's get back to the party.

Good idea. After all that talk I need a beverage.

CHAPTER 12

Book your Space City Tour today Advertisement

We all have the chance to visit Space City.
Do something out of this world.

Book your Space City Tour today.

You know that Space City is two hundred and fifty thousand kilometres long, with thousands of twenty five kilometre long rotating segments which give the effect of gravity. There are also many segment spaces occupied by factories making products for use on Earth or in space and these nonrotating areas give you the opportunity for viewing Earth and factory visits.

You can visit the Maxwell 09 spaceship factory.

You have heard the messages from Maxwell 01.

See its big brother Maxwell 09 being built.

You could be around for when it leaves in 4615.

You definitely won't be around for when it arrives at Maxwell 09 in 12100.

You have seen the videos, now walk beside the Maxwell 09 robot spaceship.

It is BIG

Be amazed at its size.

Be amazed by the swarm of robot engineers building Maxwell 09.

Book your Space City Tour today.

Or you can visit the space tugs factory.

See the Space Tugs that are protecting us.

Objects on a collision course for Earth must be deflected. See the fleet of Space Tugs waiting to do the job.

Book your Space City Tour today.

Or you can visit the Space City vertical farms at many different locations.

See the Space City vertical farms towering above you.

Pick a peach, plum or pear and enjoy a delicious snack.

Pick strawberries or blue berries or what that farm has for you to enjoy.

There is always a ripe apple, apricot, peach, pear, or your favourite fruit waiting to be picked.

See a different world.

See a different farm.

Book your Space City Tour today.

Want to visit more than one part of Space City.

Take a Space City Bus.

There is a Space City Bus waiting to whisk you from one attraction to the next.

Space City has many, many attractions for you to visit.

Sports people will find a visit to Space City a slice of the heaven your ancestors dreamed about.

Some important reminders.

You will be safe from cosmic rays. All areas are protected from too much radiation.

You will have weight. Except for the factory areas you will have weight and will walk around normally.

In factory areas your boots are made for walking as you keep to the path. You will wear a spacesuit like Neil Armstrong wore. Except enormously lighter.

Where you usually eat you will have weight and your food will sit on your plate like at home and your drink will stay in the glass.

If you have a meal in an Observation Deck you will be weightlessness but your food and drink will be in special containers for you to have a new eating experience.

Make sure you do visit an Observation Deck to see the part of the Earth you are above and see just how beautiful your home is. You will also see what has been covered by water so far.

CHAPTER 13

Hunt Location 30, Phangnga, Thailand

Well, Dad, it is only a couple of hours behind us.

Yes, Davey. You won't have trouble watching this one.

This would have to be in one of the prettiest areas.

I would say so. Lots of fishing going on there.

I wonder if it will rain, Dad.

Good chance of that, Davey. And it should be a bit warm.

They need to be good swimmers.

Yes, it will be around all the islands. But the hunters and hunted will have the same problems.

I like watching the Hunts. Both sides need to have a lot of skill to either avoid getting fish fooded or to make them fish food.

And they will need to be skilled at all aspects of water sports. I guess you are comparing it to the Arena Show.

Yes. There is not much skill shown when you have many humans wanting to run away from hungry pigs or mad dogs or angry humans.

The rebels were not just running. They did have some weapons to try to avoid being fish fooded.

I like the varied locations in each Hunt. The Arena Show is just in the Arena. A Hunt has hills and valleys and forest and rocks with a whole lot of video drones showing us what is happening.

For sure Davey. This Hunt will have action in the water or on the islands or in the caves. So you're right from that point of view. The scene is more varied.

Phangnga would have been different before the water rose.

A lot of Phuket Island is under water now. It has affected the number of tourists going there.

What would have been a beachfront hotel is now under water so it is a bit of a mess.

On the other side of the Bay a lot of Krabi will be under water.

If not all of it. The sea going up twenty metres has been bad for a lot of people.

It is just as well there are any number of construction robots to pull buildings down and move then to higher ground.

As long as you have higher ground. Some islands are not that high.

Humans like sun, sea and surf, so Phuket will always get visitors.

Even if the water does go up sixty metres there will be some of it above water. Let's hope it doesn't go that high. The carbon dioxide is proving very difficult to get out of the atmosphere.

The Earth must be as green as it has ever been. All those leaves should be doing a better job.

There are only two billion humans putting the gas back in the air, but now the numbers of all other animals are increasing a lot and there are forest fires burning around the globe.

While coal and oil are no longer the cause animals still breathe and fires still burn.

With natural means not doing the job perhaps they will start some artificial ones but so much for water rising. Phangnga has lots of places for interesting chases.

Yes Davey. I think you are going to enjoy this Hunt.

CHAPTER 14

Jimmy visits a farm

That is amazing, Ben. It is greenery from floor to roof.

Yes, Jimmy, you come around the corner and it hits you in the face. Farming Moon style.

Floor to roof chickens. Floor to roof lettuce, or cabbage. One or the other. Do you have floor to roof cows?

No, no cows. The meat of bigger animals is all made in the factory. Grown in test tubes so to speak, except the containers are enormously bigger than test tubes.

So people can buy a real egg or chicken leg but not a rump steak.

Well, it is real, it just hasn't been walking around a paddock.

I must admit, a lot of the rump steak at home is not off a cow. Cows emit too much methane which is even worse than carbon dioxide for heating up the Earth.

The Earth is not having much luck in reducing the problem gases even with the planet being all green so it needs to not do anything to make it worse.

Now the plants we see here need water and carbon dioxide and light. You certainly have a lot of light.

After the Impact people have been wary of complete dependence on solar electricity so while there is a lot of it we also have fusion reactors providing baseload power. We are underground so we need power guaranteed all the time.

With no atmosphere I suppose solar panels are affected by meteors.

Yes, small ones cause damage which the robots need to fix. Not that it happens all that frequently.

I suppose the animals in Moon City provide all the carbon dioxide.

Yep. Keep on breathing to help us out.

So this is the opposite of Earth. Here you need lots of carbon dioxide.

Yes, it is why tourists are good for the Moon. They breathe.

And you would like people burning wood for a barbeque even though we are hundreds of metres underground.

Keeping the gas at levels good for the plants is always in people's minds. So, yes, we have different priorities to those of people on Earth.

We would not want to be walking around this farm. Just as well we are on our bikes.

It is big for sure. But it can get crowded so you can't ride because people come down to see what is going on.

And pick some fruit.

There are always lots of different fruits to pick.

Like in Space City. They don't have the difficulty of seasons either.

What would you like to pick, Jimmy?

Strawberries to start with, Ben. Is that your choice too?

Good choice. Then you might like to chomp on an ear of corn. After you peel it.

Those apple trees look as though the apples are ripe.

They always have ripe apples, oranges, peaches and apricots. And different types of grapes.

I want to stay here all day, Ben. Let's eat. And I will phone Kailee about this place,

I will go and find Jenny. She was getting some things for her mum.

Hi, Kailee. We are at a Moon farm.

Hello Jimmy. What are you chomping on?

An apple. Then I am sampling the berries until I can fit no more in.

How did you get there?

We rode on bikes to an elevator and then here. We came around a corner and I was hit in the eye by floor to roof green.

I guess meeting it face to face is different to knowing about it.

For sure. It is like landing at Uluru in the middle of Australia and having this huge rock to your left, right and up. Definitely different to having seen a picture of it.

Are there any animals to see?

Just chickens, and they give us eggs as well as chicken meat from a real, live walking around animal. In a cage of course.

So people are having barbequed chicken.

Of course, that is what they are eating. There are some groups here cooking but I had not thought what was on the grill.

So Ben and Jenny are doing a good job showing you around.

For sure. It is good having a local to be with. Ben went to find Jenny. I had better go and find them. I will do that as I eat.

I will leave you to your grazing. Bye.

Bye Kailee.

CHAPTER 15

About the Celebration of Life
of Uncle Malcolm

Uncle Malcolm really had no idea who anyone was at his Celebration of Life, did he Dad.

Not at all, Davey. When your brain ceases to function it distresses everyone a great deal.

How is it that there is still no cure for dementia, Dad.

Pretty obviously the scientists have been trying to fix that problem for many, many years with no success.

But if your brain does not work you are no longer you.

That is a sad fact, Davey. It is why you have a Celebration of Life and then get fish fooded.

But while we all knew Uncle Malcolm it would have been good if he had known us.

True Davey. I think we should have a pre-Celebration of Life at yearly intervals when we get to an age where our brain might give up.

That is a really good excuse for a party every year.

Of course some people live to an age of one hundred years without a brain problem so they would certainly have a good many parties.

I think it would be better to have too many than to feel let down like we do because Uncle Malcolm did not recognise anyone.

Keep that in mind in a few years when I insist on a party every year.

You should start having parties every year for your Dad. He is getting on even if he has no brain problems.

That is where some people, including Dad, do not like the idea because it makes them think more about leaving this life behind.

I expect it was easier for many people in olden times when people thought there was a Heaven to go to after this life so they had something to look forward to.

You can see why the Church was able to influence people because they were the ones who got you into Heaven.

That was a problem with the Moslems. The idea that a martyr would have dozens of women to himself when he blew himself and others up got a lot to think it was a good idea.

Just as well that the Christians did not have the same idea. People would have been blowing themselves up all over the place.

The Octet makes us realise we need to make the best use of this life because it is the only one we are ever going to have.

It might have stopped the people in the twenties and before going to war and killing millions of people.

Especially young people who had not had any experience of life. They were not much older than me when many of them died.

Yes, I would have been very, very upset to have my boy die in a war. And some families lost several sons. It makes us so much luckier because we have the World Government and no wars. It is good that the Maxwell spaceships take all the story of Earth history so when the humans look at it they can see the only sensible government is a World Government. Of course, you also need all the jobs done by robots.

I can see that I am alive at the best time in our history. And I think we will give you a Celebration of Life starting with your next birthday Dad.

Good idea, Davey. A good excuse for a party.

CHAPTER 16

Sandy and Bill watch Hunt at 30

We have to watch it. We will see where we went, said Sandy. Yes, Phuket was a holiday to remember, said Bill.

So soon after having it in the middle of the night and now another around the same time.

Well, Hunt 30 at Phangnga is decidedly different to Hunt 34 at Albury. Just completely different.

Remember we went in submersibles around Bangkok. The temples and palaces under water and with so many buildings poking up out of it.

The waves had done an awful lot of damage. It must be heart breaking for people whose families lived there.

I just cannot imagine how they feel. And with the water still rising more of Thailand will be under water.

So many places covered so quickly. Bangkok did not move anything.

Bangkok was so low the water did not have to rise much to cover it. They used to get a lot of tourists before it went under water and they still do because there is so much to see, and it is so different to what is under water in Amsterdam and London and Shanghai.

Well, they certainly need the money. They have lost a lot of their income from shrimp farming, the industry that has been covered, and farmland.

So we did them a good turn by visiting.

That's for sure. Perhaps we should go and visit it again.

Yes, we could go north to Chiang Mai or north east to Udon Thani and Vientianne in Laos.

All with very different scenery to Birmingham, for sure.

We would see Nong Khai on the Mekong. There used to be lots of water in the river but with its source no longer as snowy as it used to be there is a lot less. I wonder if they still have boat races on the river.

That would make it a good time to visit. I would prefer December or January for up there. The temperature around Christmas is much better than any other time of the year.

Yes, remember that couple who told us of a visit in April. The town still holds the custom of throwing water around in April because it gets just so hot. A good time to stay in Birmingham unless you want to be slowly baked.

It might be enjoyable to throw water over others without them deciding to knock your block off.

Well, there were many other visitors as well as them the couple told us. Other people must also like the idea of tossing water all over the place.

It must be still worth a visit if there were a lot of people there in April. You can check if we could go around Christmas.

Good idea. So are we going to get up to see the Hunt at 30?

I think we should. They will be hunting around all those islands both in the water and out of it. It should be exciting.

Just not as exciting as the last Hunt. It will be difficult for any future Hunt to be on par with that one.

Yes, Justin Davies name will remain at the top of the list for exciting Hunts. Getting hundreds or thousands of followers to invade the Hunt area to try to rescue you is just something else.

I still can't get over what they thought they were going to do.

Where did they think they could go? This is one world.

There is just the one World Government. It controls everything. It controls everyone. It controls everywhere. It is the absolute opposite of democracy but wars are no more.

The best thing it controls is the population. There were just too many people before the Impact.

You need to be thinking about us increasing the population by one sometime.

I will. I will. I just like being able to wander off to Thailand or Space City or the Moon if we feel like it. I think Junior would put a brake on that sort of thinking.

I think we should get up to Space City or the Moon soon. I really don't like the idea of having too much radiation while I am pregnant.

They say it is safe but you are right. Accidents do happen. It would be dreadful to affect the baby's genes.

So you had better start getting on the list for Space City visits and Moon visits. Spicy shrimp soup doesn't affect a baby's genes.

I wonder if they have a different queue for potential parents.

That would be sensible. Check it out right now. We can think about the Hunt later. I want to know if we can go soon. I am getting clucky.

Right, the Hunt later and a hunt now for visits.

CHAPTER 17

Scott and Simon Arrival and vertical farms

Well Simon, that was not as bad as I expected, said Scott.
I agree. Coming down to zero speed from around ten thousand kilometres per hour I thought we were in for a torrid time.

The robot has been programmed to keep its customers happy.

Yes, good robot.

I am looking forward to picking some strawberries.

Me too. Also an apple, a peach and a plum.

You're liking that they grow fruit trees in their own little environment which means fruit of each type all year round.

Liking very much. I assume there will be vertical farms at each stop. We should have visited the one when we were over Indonesia.

They might have concentrated on tropical fruit trees. You know, mangoes, mangosteen and rambutan, they are my favourites.

With mangoes being the national fruit of India we are sure to find it here. And bananas.

We are not going to want to leave the farm. I guess they find that with a lot of their visitors.

We can get a bagful of what we want to eat and go to the viewing section and see the sea and India.

Make sure the bag is transparent. Then we can see if any fruit try to escape.

Good idea. Having apples and bananas floating around our heads would not be the way to observe India.

So far no one has invented a gravity machine. With all the scientists working on it perhaps it is just around the corner.

Well, I want to do research. Maybe you can join me and we will invent it.

Too bad that they have been trying for thousands of years. I don't think I will be the one.

It would be handy though. Weightlessness is uncomfortable.

And it would mean the sections of Space City would not have to rotate.

Of course if it made gravity it could also cancel it out. Great for moving a pyramid around the place.

The Space City Bus would not have to rotate either. Or the Moon Bus.

You had better join me to get working on it as soon as we finish our trip and we start tertiary studies.

We would need to be near good Physics labs. The material can be put in my brain but we need to handle the equipment and there will not be many places with the gear we will need.

Right. You can do something about Education Inputs later but first we need to invent a gravity machine.

Bring your bag. There is our Space City Shuttle to the hotel.

So will you consider Physics first, education later?

It sounds like an interesting plan. The equipment will be a decider I think. Of course I need to have them agree to me changing. But not to invent a gravity machine.

No. I guess that would be a stretch to imagine we would be that lucky.

You have talked about developing better spaceship engines. That would be really useful. I still need permission.

That won't be a problem Your scores are at the top. You can study whatever interests you. I'm really looking forward to working with you.

Me too. This trip has been great. To work together would work really well.

So, hotel check-in, then farmyard frolics, then eat while we talk about getting to other planets a few hundred years sooner.

And this must be the hotel. Looks good.

It does. Let's join the queue.

CHAPTER 18

Kevin and Julie in London

Well, here we are Julie. The train certainly moves. It does. The boat leaves from Pier 06. It will take us to the Abbey.

I would have been reluctant to move England's history too. The Abbey holds a lot of English history. But with the water still rising it is going to be under water soon.

Those walls they have around it look very tall. I guess they have to be worried about waves crashing over them if they were lower.

I thought we would not have so much company. This place is crowded.

Yes, when they said there was a walkway you could follow to see the likes of Newton and Darwin and the Queen Elizabeths being removed to go to Birmingham I thought one walkway.

There are dozens. And they are all crowded.

We all love the Abbey. We don't have to work. We can all come to look. I wonder if it is like this every day?

Westminster Abbey has been a favourite place to see for people from all around the world forever. To have it going under water with the rest of London is really bad.

If this queue doesn't speed up we will be going under water too.

London had a population of millions. They have all lost their homes.

It is just as well the Earth has population control. If humans had continued to breed like rabbits I don't know where they would have put them all.

One thing about having construction robots. Tell them "Build a new apartment building there" and a swarm of them have it built by next week; or that is what it seems anyway.

There were many forests of apartment buildings we could see from the train. It is better to go up than out and destroy all the forest.

The Earth can support two billion humans forever. Of course there are also the people in Space City and on the Moon who don't count as being on the Earth. When the water goes down they will have people back in London. Robots will have to build it all again. We just don't want humans everywhere.

They were taking over everywhere until the China Impact. Losing a few billion was bad for them but good for the planet.

Yes, if the human numbers had been controlled there would not have been the need to burn so much coal so we would not have Cambridge under water today.

And parts of Chester. We must get over there soon. As the water keeps going up more of it gets covered. That is some more of our history being destroyed.

Manchester is dry at present but when it gets to sixty metres Manchester is submerged.

It's too bad they did not have the Octet back then. The religions making people think they were a vastly superior animal that did not need to curb its increase in numbers was extremely unfortunate.

Yes. People should have had the attitude of the Sioux Indians from North America. They had a better relationship with the other animals.

Having the World Government means that there is no conflict between nations because there are no nations.

Problem people like Justin Davies are the exception rather than the rule.

Yes, we do not have sections of the world population thinking they need to increase their numbers to deter invaders.

Well, when a lot of the people we are seeing extracted from the ground here were alive they certainly had conflict but numbers did not increase hugely until machines were working.

Yes, if it had not been for the Octet then having robots do all the work would have meant humans had nothing to do but work at procreating.

Religions have a lot to answer for. Those people, or expeople, down there would have all believed in a religion.

Those robots are getting things done at a pretty fast rate. When all the coffins are out the bricks follow. There are robots everywhere.

They work all day and all night. At this rate we will be visiting Westminster Abbey in Birmingham very soon.

Just as long as there are less people wanting to do it when we do rather than like the present.

So many people. Come on. We will go on that submersible tour of London before we go home.

Good. I've seen enough. I'm glad we came.

Me too. Too bad there are many other places we could see being moved as well.

Right. Let's find our sub.

CHAPTER 19

Jimmy talks about Ben's win

Well, Kailee. As they say, practice makes perfect. We Earth guys have had very little practice in Moon conditions and did we get whomped.

Hi Jimmy. You mean Ben and company really won everything?

Not everything. Just the things I was wanting to win.

Wait until you get them down here and you can show them what skiing is like in the Alps.

Thanks for your confidence. Mine is shot to pieces.

The Moon conditions are just so different to Earth with Moon's low gravity.

True. They probably won't even be able to walk if they don't get down there soon.

How much longer are Ben and Jenny there?

Not long. Their parents love it here but they know the kids need Earth gravity.

So tomorrow you go walkabout on the surface.

Yes, and Ben and Jenny are joining the group.

Have they been mixing with your team members?

For sure. Every night it has been a party. Possibly has something to do with my success as well as the gravity.

So the coach knew about the partying?

They were in all of them. The whole event has been as much about socialising as competing.

I suppose the Moon men will be back with those coaches in the near future.

And women. There are a lot of sports minded Moon women.

Good for keeping muscles in shape.

It is going to be a bit different walking around on the surface in a Moon suit. I am used to weighing a bit over ten kilograms.

Armstrong and company had suits weighing as much as they did. Do you know how heavy the suit is?

It hasn't come up. I guess it will be about the same. I will still be able to hop around like they did.

Make sure you send me a copy of the video of your small steps.

That reminds me. We go to see his footprint.

You mean Neil Armstrong's?

Yes. Because there is no air the footprints are there forever. We will go and see them and the flag. And all the other stuff.

So you will be in Moon suits again.

No. They have a dome around it. The actual stuff from the first landing is not in the dome but it makes it more comfortable for us tourists.

How do you get there?

A tourist rocket of some sort. I will have to tell you about that later. I have no idea.

I suppose that a lot of people want to visit the site of a human's first step on the Moon.

Evidently it is a big attraction. I suppose there might even be a train right there.

Having robot miners that can do all the work it would make sense to have a tunnel to the site. You have got trains to all the other cities.

I guess I'll be telling you about my train trip when I call you tomorrow. Bye.

Bye, Jimmy. Have a good walk.

Thanks.

CHAPTER 20

12 day Moon tour for Stage 12 Physics students

Day 1 Saturday September 7, 4576
Meet at Albury Airport.
Fly to Indonesia 2 Space Elevator.
Transfer to Java One Hotel.
O/N Java One Hotel
Day 2 Sunday September 8, 4576
Full Breakfast.
Transfer to Indonesia 2 Space Elevator Terminal.
Travel up the Indonesia 2 Space Elevator to the Space City.
Lunch and dinner in the Space Elevator.
O/N Space City Excelsior Hotel
Day 3 Monday September 9, 4576
Full Breakfast.
Tour of Space City factory to see Maxwell 09 spaceship being built.
Lunch
Visit Research Centre
Physics experiments in the weightless laboratory.
Dinner at Earth View Restaurant

Return to Space City Excelsior Hotel.

O/N Space City Excelsior Hotel

Day 4 Tuesday September 10, 4576

Full Breakfast.

Visit a vertical farm.

Lunch observing Earth in the weightless section. View the Earth and take photos of your home.

Physics experiments in the weightless laboratory.

Dinner at Earth View Restaurant

Return to Space City Excelsior Hotel.

O/N Space City Excelsior Hotel

Day 5 Wednesday September 11, 4576

Full Breakfast.

Transfer to Moon Bus Terminal

Moon Bus to Moon City.

Lunch and dinner in the Moon Bus

O/N Hilton Moon City

Day 6 Thursday September 12, 4576

Full Breakfast.

Tour of Moon City

Lunch at Earth View Restaurant

Visit Lunar Research Centre

Experiments in lunar gravity.

Dinner at Earth View Restaurant

O/N Hilton Moon City

Day 7 Friday September 13, 4576

Full Breakfast.

Experiments in lunar gravity.

Lunch

Walk on the surface of the Moon for one hour.

Transfer to train to Neil Armstrong City

Travel to Neil Armstrong City

Transfer to First Landing Hotel

Dinner at hotel.

O/N First Landing Hotel

Day 8 Saturday September 14, 4576

Full Breakfast.

Visit Neil Armstrong Memorial Dome to see the first footprints on the Moon in 1969.

Other attractions to see include the flag, lunar module and various vehicles and other equipment from later landings. Some of these will be within the Dome.

Lunch in the Dome at the Earth View Restaurant

Transfer to train to Moon City for return journey.

Dinner at the hotel.

O/N Hilton Moon City

Day 9 Sunday September 15, 4576

Full Breakfast.

Physics experiments in lunar gravity.

Take a second walk on the surface of the Moon for one hour.

Lunch

Free time to see Moon City.

Dinner at Earth View Restaurant

O/N Hilton Moon City

Day 10 Monday September 16, 4576

Full Breakfast.

Transfer to Moon Bus Terminal

Travel on the Moon Bus to Space City.

Transfer to Hilton Space City

Dinner at the hotel.

O/N Hilton Space City

Day 11 Tuesday September 17, 4576

Full Breakfast.

Travel down the Indonesia 2 Space Elevator to the Earth.

Transfer to Java One Hotel.
O/N Java One Hotel
Day 12 Wednesday September 18, 4576
Full Breakfast.
Transfer to airport.
Fly home.

Lightning Source UK Ltd.
Milton Keynes UK
UKHW010140230422
401939UK00007B/386/J